"Pick up your glass, and drink to my success."

"My tender has been accepted for the new steel plant," Vince continued, his voice triumphant.

Now her father would have to sell everything to repay the loan. This was the final blow.

Their eyes locked in silent battle for interminable seconds before Cara raised her glass with an air of defiance. "I won't drink to your success, Vince, but I'll drink to the sincere wish that your desire for revenge will at last be satisfied and you rid yourself of the hatred that is destroying you."

She swallowed a mouthful of the bubbling liquid. "Now, if you'll excuse me, I'm going to see my father."

Cara drew in an anguished breath that sounded more like a sob. She loved Vince, but he was tearing her in two.

Books by Yvonne Whittal

These books may be available at your local bookseller.

Don't miss any of our special offers. Write to us at the following address for information on our newest releases.

Harlequin Reader Service
P.O. Box 52040, Phoenix, AZ 85072-2040
Canadian address: P.O. Box 2800, Postal Station A,
5170 Yonge St., Willowdale, Ont. M2N 6J3

YVONNE WHITTAL

the devil's pawn

Harlequin Books

TORONTO • NEW YORK • LONDON
AMSTERDAM • PARIS • SYDNEY • HAMBURG
STOCKHOLM • ATHENS • TOKYO • MILAN

Harlequin Presents first edition April 1985
ISBN 0-373-10782-X

Original hardcover edition published in 1984
by Mills & Boon Limited

CHAPTER ONE

THE sound of raised voices coming from the direction of the study made Cara Lloyd pause in the spacious hall and glance at the grandfather clock with its ornately carved stinkwood casing. It was after ten o'clock in the evening, and concern puckered her smooth brow between the dark, winged eyebrows. Who could possibly have had the audacity to call at this late hour to discuss business with her father?

She turned towards the kitchen, but the heated and prolonged argument behind that closed door made her pause a second time. It was an unspoken rule in her father's home not to interfere in his business affairs, but his raised, clearly distraught voice made the frown deepen between her brows, and she crossed the thickly carpeted hall to listen in unashamedly to the conversation being conducted behind that panelled door.

'Twelve months, that's all I'm asking for,' her father pleaded. 'Please give me another twelve months?'

'No way, Lloyd,' a deep voice replied cuttingly. 'Our agreement was for eighteen months, and that's it. Either you pay up by midday this Saturday, or you're out of business completely.'

The threat was unmistakable, and Cara's curiosity intensified when her father exploded, 'That's inhuman!'

'That's *justice*, Lloyd,' that deep, unfamiliar voice snarled with a savagery that made Cara tremble. 'You called the tune once, but now the time has come for you to dance to mine.'

5

'Oh, my God!' David Lloyd groaned, and the sound of utter defeat in his voice was too much for Cara to bear. She opened the door without knocking and stepped into the study with its oak-panelled walls to find her father seated behind his desk with his head in his hands.

'Dad?' she queried softly, her voice husky with concern, but a movement beside the French windows made her turn, and her glance collided with narrowed grey eyes that reminded her of the film of ice in the bird bath on a cold wintry morning.

Recognition was like an unpleasant shiver of shock tripping across her nerve ends, and her pulse began to drum loudly against her temples. She knew this man with the sun-bleached hair and tanned, rugged features. His tall, wide-shouldered frame had been imposing at a distance, but now it seemed to shrink the size of the spacious study to almost that of a closet.

Cara wrenched her eyes from his and turned to her father in a valiant, but unsuccessful, attempt to ignore the man whose presence had disturbed and disrupted her composure so often during the past year at local functions and parties. 'Is everything all right, Dad?' she asked, looking down into David Lloyd's pale face.

'We're discussing business, Cara,' he reminded her sharply, but he softened the rebuke by adding gently, 'Don't concern yourself, my dear.'

She hesitated, her tawny eyes studying him with grave uncertainty, but the set of his mouth told her that this was not the moment to contradict him, and she turned reluctantly towards the door.

'Just a minute!' Her fingers curled nervously into her palms at the sound of that deep, commanding voice, and she turned beside her father's desk to face the man approachng her. Cara's slender body was of average height, but this man dwarfed her completely, and her insides quivered with something she attributed to fear as he extended a hand towards her. 'I'm Vince Steiner.'

'As if I didn't know that,' she thought with unaccustomed cynicism. Everyone in Murrayville knew of the blond giant at the head of the Steiner Engineering & Construction Company. He had offices in most of the major cities, commuting between them in a ten-seater, privately owned jet, so Cara had been told, but for some inexplicable reason he had chosen to take a personal interest in the erection of the local steel plant which was being undertaken by his company, and for this purpose he had moved to Murrayville. His appearance was savagely masculine, making it difficult to forget him even after the briefest glimpse. Women literally swooned at his feet, and conniving mothers had set their sights on him as a future son-in-law, but Vince Steiner had remained aloof from their persistent invitations, and the beautiful Chantal Webber from Johannesburg had finally dashed their hopes with her frequent visits to his palatial home which he had rented on the outskirts of the town.

Cara's small, slender hand disappeared into his, and the cool rough texture sent an electrifying warmth surging through her which was infinitely more disturbing than the many times she had seen him observing her at functions over the past year. They had never been introduced. In a town like Murrayville it was taken for granted that everyone knew everyone else, and to date they had always had the length of a room between them. This accounted for her not recognising his voice, but his devouring eyes had spoken volumes on each occasion their glances had met in the past, and Cara had gone to great lengths to maintain a comfortable distance between them.

She extricated her hand from his with care, her fingers tingling with the memory of his touch, and she turned from him to see the deepening frown between her father's busy brows. 'Dad, what's going on?' she questioned him determinedly.

David Lloyd's mouth tightened disapprovingly, but it was Vince Steiner who broke the brief, tense silence in the room.

'Are you going to tell her, Lloyd, or shall I?' he demanded with icy disdain, and Cara saw her father's face go a shade paler.

'I don't want my wife and my daughter involved in this.'

'Whether you want it, or not, they're going to be involved, so you might as well tell her,' Vince Steiner argued, the resonant timbre of his voice vibrating with impatience and anger, and Cara was once again aware of a distant threat hovering behind his statement.

'Dad?' she questioned huskily, and she experienced the first icy blast of fear when she darted a brief glance at Vince Steiner's harsh, unrelenting features.

David Lloyd sat frozen behind his desk for interminable seconds, his face pale and distraught, but he cracked finally under the mental pressure brought to bear on him.

'There has been a slump in the building trade these past two years,' he explained tonelessly, sagging in his chair as if his body had suddenly become boneless. 'Circumstances forced me to approach Mr Steiner. He had the monopoly on the erection of the steel plant out of town, and I hoped that he could engage my company as a sub-contractor, but he turned me down.'

Cara shot an angry, disillusioned glance at the man beside her. So Vince Steiner was the sort who kicked a man when he was down. The look in his cold grey eyes told her that he was perfectly aware of what she thought of him, but it also told her that he could not care less.

'There's more to it than that, Lloyd,' he corrected her father harshly and, turning to confront Cara, he concluded her father's brief explanation. 'Your father approached me again eighteen months ago. He needed money, and I gave it to him.'

Shock and dismay made her draw a sharp breath, and her eyes pleaded with her father when their glances met. 'Is this true?' she managed jerkily.

'Yes,' David Lloyd confirmed, his hand trembling as he took out his handkerchief to wipe the beads of perspiration off his forehead. 'I had already sold my business premises to make ends meet, and the house has been heavily mortgaged. I tried to get a loan from the bank to keep me going until my business improved, but I had nothing to offer as security, so they turned down my application.'

'You took money from Mr Steiner?' she demanded incredulously, still finding it impossible to believe that her father could have done such a thing, and David Lloyd sagged further into his chair until he looked like a tired old man of eighty instead of a sprightly sixty.

'I had no other choice, Cara. I was desperate when he made the offer.'

'And you don't have the money to pay back that loan?' she grasped the situation at last, and her father confirmed this with a brief nod of his head before he elaborated.

'To pay back the loan means that I would have to sell this house and everything in it.'

'You can't sell this house!' Cara gasped in something akin to horror. 'It would destroy Mother if you did that!'

David Lloyd mopped again at his perspiring brow and gestured helplessly. 'I know, Cara, but it seems I may have no other alternative.'

'What a touching little scene,' Vince Steiner sneered, shattering the ensuing silence, and Cara turned on him, her tawny eyes fiery with anger. 'Can't you see what you're doing to my father? Have you no feelings at all, Mr Steiner?'

His eyes were cool in their assessment of her, and his glance travelled with slow deliberation from her dark, glossy hair, piled into an elegant knot in the nape of her slender neck, down to her sandalled feet. He was nothing if not thorough, and Cara was aware yet again of that feeling that her clothes were no barrier against the blatant sexuality of his probing eyes. She felt hot and embarrassed, as if she had been stripped mentally down to her skin, and his insolent, faintly sensuous smile told her that he was well aware of her reaction. He had done this to her before many times in the past, and she had not reached the age of twenty-four without encountering a few desirous glances, but none had affected her as alarmingly as Vince Steiner's. He wanted her, and this time he was making no secret of it. The knowledge repulsed and excited her simultaneously, and she despised herself for the latter as she hid the effect he was having on her behind a cool, haughty exterior.

He raised a large, sun-browned hand and fingered a stray curl beside her ear with a confidence that bordered on arrogance. 'At this moment I'm having very strong feelings.'

His contradiction of her accusation startled her, but she would not give him the satisfaction of witnessing her emotional distress and, without moving away from him, she said icily, 'Don't touch me!'

His smile deepened until deep grooves formed in his

lean cheeks. White teeth flashed contrastingly against his tanned features, but there was something malevolent in that smile when he lowered his hand and turned his attention to her father.

'I think the solution to your problem is right here, Lloyd,' he said smoothly, gesturing towards Cara.

'*No!*' Ashen-faced, David Lloyd leapt to his feet behind his desk. 'Leave Cara out of this!'

Cara's quick mind had grasped the meaning behind Vince Steiner's statement, but a part of her stubbornly refused to believe it, and exasperation boiled up inside of her. 'Would someone please explain what's going on?'

'There is nothing to explain, and the subject is closed,' her father barked, gesturing towards the door. 'Leave us now, Cara.'

Not even Cara's mother disobeyed when David Lloyd used that tone of voice, and Cara turned once again towards the door to leave the study.

'Cara!' Her name on Vince Steiner's lips sent a sharp, curious tremor racing through her. Something warned her to ignore his unspoken command to remain, but a force stronger than her own made her pause at the door to glance back at him. His square jaw was set in a harsh, unrelenting line, and his grey eyes were piercingly intent on her face. 'Would you help your father if you could?'

'Leave Cara out of this, Steiner!' her father exploded before Cara could formulate a suitable reply, but Vince Steiner was undaunted by her father's angry stance.

'I asked you a question,' he reminded Cara, 'and I'm waiting for an answer.'

'Don't say anything, Cara!' her father instructed, a ring of frantic desperation in his voice. 'For God's sake, don't say anything!'

The perspiration was literally running in rivulets down her father's forehead, but Vince Steiner was hatefully cool and calm. He was in complete control, and he knew it. Cara's dislike deepened, and loyalty to her father dictated her actions when she stepped away from the door.

'Dad, I love you, and I care about what happens to you, and. . . .' Ignoring the plea in her father's eyes, she turned towards the man who had observed her with that strange intensity during the past few seconds. 'Yes, Mr Steiner, I would help my father if I could.'

'In that case I have a proposition to put to you.' The tension in the room spiralled higher as he took his time lighting a cigarette, and Cara thought she had never before seen anyone ooze such supreme confidence. It frightened her, but she would not give in to the thoughts which were beginning to race through her mind. 'Your father wants me to give him twelve months grace to repay the loan. I'll do that, but in exchange for my leniency I shall require certain security.'

'Here it comes,' she thought. 'He wants me to be his mistress.' She could no longer deny to herself that this was what she had suspected when he had referred to her as the solution to her father's problem, but she feigned innocence when she asked: 'What form of security do you need, Mr Steiner?'

'Marry me, Cara, and your father can have those twelve months he's been begging me for.'

Cara felt as if the air had been driven from her body by a giant hand squeezing her lungs ruthlessly. Of all things she had never expected Vince Steiner to propose *marriage* as the solution. He was nearer forty than thirty, and there was about him a certain aura that suggested he was a man who preferred his freedom to the bondage of marriage. That was how she had summed him up, and to suggest marriage on this unheard of basis was totally ludicrous.

'You must be mad!' she accused sharply, fear heightening that attractive husky quality in her voice.

'I suggest you both think it over, and I shall call again tomorrow evening for your answer.' Vince Steiner crushed his half-smoked cigarette into the copper ashtray on the desk, and Cara was beginning to detest the calm arrogance of the man as he inclined his head briefly in their direction. 'Goodnight, Lloyd . . . Cara.'

He chose the French windows to make his exit, but seconds—or was it hours later—she could still feel his dominant, threatening presence in the silent room.

'He couldn't have been serious,' Cara brushed aside Vince Steiner's proposal, but her face was now as white as her father's. 'It could only have been a joke.'

David Lloyd sat down heavily behind his desk and shook his grey head. 'I'm afraid he meant it, Cara.'

She groped blindly for the chair beside her, and sat down quickly before her legs gave way totally beneath her. She would not believe it! She *could* not believe it! There had to be another solution to her father's problem, and she would find it. Vince Steiner was not the only man with confidence in himself, and she would prove this to him.

Her frightened tremors began to subside, and she faced her father with admirable calmness across the width of his desk. 'How did you land yourself in this mess, Dad?'

'I told you, there has been a slump in the building trade, and it didn't help when Steiner's company succeeded in acquiring the contract for the new steel plant being erected here,' David Lloyd explained tiredly. 'When I failed to get the contract for the plant, I put in a tender for the houses which are now being erected for the steel company's staff, but Steiner has the monopoly on that as well.'

Cara did not need her father to tell her of Vince Steiner's success. The smaller construction companies in the area had crumbled swiftly during the past year until her father's company was the only one left. The Steiner Engineering & Construction Company was too powerful to outbid, that was how the spokesmen for the other companies had explained their disintegration, but none of them had been as ruthlessly destroyed as her father's company was about to be.

'I know how powerful the Steiner Company is,' Cara argued, 'but that still doesn't explain why you needed a loan. Surely you had built up a sizeable amount in capital over the years?'

She had never seen her father perspire the way he was perspiring now, and she waited with characteristic patience while he mopped his brow once again.

'Without work there was no money coming in,' he explained at length. 'It takes money to continue living in the style to which one is accustomed, and when the business took a dive I had to delve into the capital to make ends meet.'

It was a feasible excuse, but Cara had a feeling that her father was hiding something from her. 'We were, in other words, living beyond our means, but if you told Mother I'm sure she would have done something about cutting down on the expenses.'

'I didn't want her to know,' David Lloyd groaned, burying his face in his hands for a moment before they dropped back into his lap, and the eyes that met Cara's were glazed. 'I always hoped that the situation would improve, but then Steiner moved in, and one by one the smaller construction companies faded away. I knew it would happen to me as well, but I continued to hope that I was wrong.'

Cara got to her feet and paced the floor restlessly, and her slender body moved with a natural, fluid grace. Her delicate features were pale and her thoughts revolved in chaotic circles. She could not erase Vince Steiner's features from her mind, and she suppressed a shudder when his unacceptable proposal forced its way to supremacy in her thoughts. She had never before met someone so aggressively male, and she had a nasty suspicion that he would be totally ruthless in getting what he wanted out of life. He could have been more lenient with her father, but she had sensed in his manner an undercurrent of something she was as yet unaware of, and she wondered if she would ever know the true reason behind his obvious determination to break her father so completely.

'What makes you think you will be able to pay back the loan in a year from now?' she questioned her father in the hope that he might say something which would offer her an escape route.

'The steel company has asked for tenders for a second plant they want to erect about fifteen kilometres from here, and there is a good chance that I might get it, but I won't know for at least another two months.'

'And if you don't get it?'

She knew the answer already, it was there in the pallor of his face, but the question had been wrung from her with something close to desperation.

'If I don't get the contract, then I'll be ruined financially,' her father informed her, and his hands shook when he pushed his fingers uncharacteristically through his hair. 'We will have to sell this house, and I doubt if your mother will ever forgive me for that.'

Cara could imagine how her mother would feel about selling the home she had known for so many years, and she could also imagine what it would do to her mother to have to part with the various pieces of antique furniture which she had collected with such loving care.

'I don't think we should tell Mother about this ... not yet, anyway,' Cara suggested, and her father nodded tiredly.

'I don't know what I'm going to do if Steiner refuses to extend our agreement, Cara.'

He had perhaps not meant it to sound like a plea for help, but Cara felt as if she had been driven into a corner. If Vince Steiner was to be taken seriously, then she had it within her power to save the situation for both her father and her mother. The price she would have to pay for his leniency made her shudder, but she found herself considering his proposal of marriage seriously for the first time.

Cara was happy in her job as Librarian at the local library. With her degree in literature she found it an absorbing and interesting occupation, but her concentration left much to be desired the following morning. Her mind was occupied with the problem of saving her home while at the same time escaping the clutches of Vince Steiner, and her young assistant, Nancy de Witt, glanced at her curiously on several occasions when she had made blatant errors in filing the membership cards.

'Why don't you take a break, Miss Lloyd,' Nancy suggested that afternoon when Cara's carelessness during the day had obviously led her to believe that her superior was tired. 'I'll cope in here and, if there are any queries, I'll refer them to you.'

Cara hesitated momentarily, then she nodded abruptly. 'I'll be in my office if you need me.'

She sighed with relief when she sat down behind her

desk, but her glance rested on the pile of correspondence in front of her, and she groaned inwardly. She simply could not cope while her mind leapt about like a frantic hare seeking an escape hole to jump into, but she pulled the pile of correspondence towards her and managed to draft a few letters in reply before there was a light tap on her door.

'Come in, Nancy,' she called absently, putting down her pen and raising her glance. The door was opened, but her eyes widened beneath her delicately arched brows when she found herself looking up into a pair of ice-grey eyes. 'Mr Steiner!'

He stepped into her small office, and the sheer length and breadth of him dwarfed its cluttered interior into the claustrophobic size of a cupboard when he closed the door behind him. 'Miss de Witt said you wouldn't object to being disturbed.'

Disturbed was a mild word compared to what she felt at that moment. Her nerves were jangling as if she had been connected to an alarm, and her mind was a frantic mess of thoughts and impressions that left her staring rather stupidly at Vince Steiner for a moment. The cut of his immaculate brown suit accentuated the width of his shoulders and the leanness of his hips. His thigh muscles strained against the confining cloth of his trousers and, when she happened to glance at his large hands, the words of an old song came to mind.

One fist of iron, the other of steel,
If the right one don't get you, then the left one will.

There was a threat in those words, and this was not the first time Cara had sensed that thread of steel in this man's bearing. He could break anyone as easily as he could break a twig between those strong fingers with the clean, neatly clipped nails, and this was not a very reassuring thought while she struggled to gather her scattered wits about her.

'Won't you please sit down,' she heard herself saying politely in a voice that sounded incredibly cool and calm while everything within her wanted to scream abuse at him. He seated himself in the chair facing her across the small desk, and she laced her trembling fingers together in her lap. 'How can I help you?'

His mocking eyes trailed from her high cheekbones down to her full, sensitive mouth. 'You know why I'm here.'

Cara should have anticipated something like this, but instead she was totally unprepared for it, and she felt herself shrinking visibly from the decision she knew she had to make.

'I thought you would be coming to our home this evening for your answer.' She spoke evasively, her face pale, and her body rigid with antagonism and dislike.

'I don't think you fully understand the seriousness of the matter, and I am here to stress the fact that I meant what I said last night.' Vince Steiner's cold eyes held hers with an effortless ease that frightened her, and she felt like a trapped animal with no way to escape. 'Marry me, and your father can have the extra twelve months to repay his loan.'

'Why are you so hard on him, Mr Steiner?' she questioned him with an unconscious plea in her eyes. 'Why can't you be a little lenient and give him the extra time he requires?'

'I have my reasons.' His hand dipped into the inside pocket of his jacket and he took out a gold cigarette case. 'One of those reasons is that he signed an agreement to the effect that he would repay his loan on or before this coming Saturday.'

Cara watched him light a cigarette, and decided to

probe a little deeper into the mysterious hold this man had on her father. 'How much did my father borrow from you?'

A cloud of smoke was ejected forcibly between his chiselled lips and directed towards the ceiling while his narrowed, speculative eyes met hers. 'A quarter of a million.'

If Cara had not been seated at that moment she dreaded to think what might have happened. The room spun crazily for several seconds before it seemed to right itself, and she caught the fleshy part of her lower lip sharply between her teeth as if she subconsciously hoped the pain of it would help to steady her. A quarter of a million rand was a fortune, and it did not surprise her now that this man was exerting pressure on her father.

'Mr Steiner. . . .' She swallowed convulsively and clasped her hands a little tighter in her lap. 'Is there no other way we can solve this problem?'

'There is,' he smiled twistedly, tapping his cigarette ash into the ashtray she pushed towards him. 'The sale of your home and the furniture in it might only just collect the amount owing to me.'

'How easily you say that, Mr Steiner,' she accused, her wide, attractively curved mouth tightening. 'Do you have any notion of the sentimental value one attaches to those things one has collected over the years to form a part of one's home?'

'I'm not a sentimental man, Cara.' His use of her name once again sent that odd tremor racing through her, but she shrugged it off with distaste when he continued speaking. 'I deal with facts and figures, and I learnt a long time ago that sentimentality has no place in business.'

He was as unrelenting as the concrete wall behind

him, she could see this now, and nothing would divert him from the stance he had taken. His rigid, unbending manner frightened her, and it was fear that drove her to her feet to stare out of the window into the street. The children were playing in the park. She could see them laughing as they propelled themselves with their bodies to urge the swing to higher realms, and she envied them in that moment. They were so carefree and happy, and she would have given anything to be one of them for just a few brief hours.

There was something she had to know, but she could not bear to face the man seated in the chair behind her, so she kept her back turned rigidly towards him. 'If I— If I agree to marry you. . . .'

'If you agree to marry me, and your father repays his loan within the next twelve months, then I shall naturally free you from our marriage,' Vince Steiner elaborated in his deep-throated voice.

'And if he can't repay the loan?' she asked, holding her breath for an agonised second.

'You shall be free after twelve months no matter what happens.' She felt certain that his eyes were roaming over her body, probing beneath the neat grey skirt and crisp white blouse, and she turned to see that her suspicions were confirmed. His eyes flicked over her lazily, lingering deliberately on her small breasts and, to her complete dismay, she felt their thrusting response as if he had actually touched her. The smile that curved his mouth told her that her reaction had not escaped his notice, and the blood rushed into her cheeks to make her furious eyes look feverishly bright. 'I think I shall have had my money's worth out of you after twelve months,' he added, filling her with a shuddering revulsion and something else she could not define.

'You disgust me, Mr Steiner!' she spat out the words.

'I'm a man of thirty-eight, Cara,' he mocked her, crushing his cigarette into the ashtray and rising to his feet to tower over her. 'Did you think I would propose a marriage in name only?'

The powerful force of his masculinity overwhelmed her to the extent that she was aware of her femininity in a way she had never been before, and she tried to back away from him only to have the windowsill dig into her waist. 'Do you think I have no feelings?' she demanded defensively.

'I'm quite sure you have feelings, but I've watched you closely during this past year, and you hide your feelings well behind that cool as marble exterior of yours.' His cold eyes came alive with mockery and hateful anticipation as his glance flicked over her. 'You have intrigued me for some time, and now I will have the opportunity of getting to know everything about you.'

'You are assuming arrogantly that I will marry you,' she snapped accusingly, but her accusation bounced off him like a rubber ball against a wall.

'When you walked into your father's study last night you paved the way for your own future, and you gave me an exciting glimpse of what lay beneath that cool surface you display to the world,' he voiced the price she would have to pay for her curiosity and concern. 'It has made me curious to know more.'

'What would have happened if I hadn't walked in on your discussion last night?'

His square jaw hardened. 'Your father would have been making arrangements this minute to sell your home.'

She knew that he meant it, and she disliked him in that moment with an intensity that simmered within her like a volcano. 'You have given me a glimpse into your character as well, Mr Steiner, and I don't particularly like what I see. You're determined to monopolise the building industry in this area, and you don't really care whom you crush in the process of climbing your particular ladder of success. It's a despicable trait, and one which will never reward you with a shred of happiness.'

'I'm not looking for happiness,' he corrected harshly. 'What I want is justice, and if my methods of acquiring it don't appeal to you, then that's just too bad.'

'Justice?' she gasped the word incredulously, her tawny eyes flashing up at him angrily. 'What has my father ever done to you that you should want to crush him so completely in your search for so-called justice?'

'Isn't it enough that he could have taken a loan from me, and then not want to repay it within the specified time?' he demanded bitingly.

'It's not a criminal offence to be in financial difficulties,' she reminded this man who seemed to have an answer for everything.

'It can become a criminal offence if I decide to take the necessary legal steps,' he threatened, and Cara went cold at the thought.

'My father is not reluctant to repay you,' she argued, forcing herself to remain calm despite her growing fears. 'If you took legal action then you would have to agree in court to receiving a monthly repayment of the loan.'

'You obviously don't know much about your father's financial predicament,' he laughed, leaning back against her desk and folding his arms across his broad chest. 'You and your mother have been existing on your father's reputation in this town for the past two years. He owes everybody money; the butcher, the baker, you name it. No one wants to take action because they know him too well and, if he can't pay his ordinary debts every month, how do you think he is going to repay the loan he accepted from me. Oh, no, Cara, to sue him is not the solution, as I see it. I'll give him another twelve months with you as security, but in the end he will have to sell up and admit he's a failure.'

'He won't have to do that,' the words spilled unwisely from her lips.

'Oh?' Vince Steiner remarked, his eyes narrowed and intent upon her white face, and she shook her head, indicating that she was not going to say more, but he seemed capable of reading her like a book. 'Don't tell me your father has put in a tender for the new steel plant?' Her expression must have given her away because he laughed derisively. 'He can forget about it.'

'If my father has put in a tender,' she said cautiously, 'then there is a strong possibility he will get the contract.'

'I wouldn't bet on that,' Vince Steiner snorted disparagingly.

'Why not?'

His mouth twisted in a hateful smile. 'I have also tendered for that steel plant, and I'm confident that I'll get the contract.'

Cara had never lost her temper before, but this man was succeeding admirably where everyone else had failed, and she clenched her hands at her sides to prevent herself from striking him. 'Isn't it enough that you got the contract for the first steel plant? Do you have to try and snatch this one away from my father as well?'

He raised a sardonic eyebrow. 'I'm not doing any snatching, believe me. I put in a tender, and we will have to wait and see who gets the contract.'

'I think you're the devil himself,' she hissed, her eyes

dark with an inner fury, and his harsh laughter made her shake with the desire to lash out at him physically.

'Tell your father I'll call around at eight this evening, and I shall want an answer one way or the other.'

He strode out of her office and closed the door behind him, but his threatening ultimatum hovered like a dark cloud in the office for some minutes after he had gone.

Cara stood there trembling with a fury that made her breath come jerkily over her parted lips. She was trapped! To protect her father, and to save the home her mother loved so much, she would have to marry Vince Steiner, and everything within her cried out in fierce protest at the mere thought of it.

CHAPTER TWO

'I STILL can't understand why you had to rush into marriage in this abominable way,' Lilian Lloyd muttered disapprovingly as she zipped Cara into her dress, and their eyes, very similar in colour, met in the dressing-table mirror. 'You could have announced your engagement, and in a few weeks from now you could have had a respectable church wedding to which we could have invited our family and friends.'

Cara had seldom hidden anything of importance from her mother, and habit was her enemy at that moment. To prevent the truth from spilling out she clenched her teeth so tightly that her jaw ached. Bitterness rose like gall within her, but she played out the charade which had begun a few days ago when she had agreed to marry Vince Steiner to save her parents from losing everything they held most dear.

She smiled forcibly into the eyes observing her so anxiously in the mirror. 'Mother, I know that a ceremony in the magistrate's office was not exactly what you had envisaged for me, but both Vince and I want it this way.'

'It's indecent, that's what it is, and I wasn't even aware that you knew each other,' Lilian complained, her grey head only just visible behind Cara's in the mirror when she fastened the hook above the zip, then she swung Cara round and looked her up and down with a new kind of anxiety. 'You're not pregnant, are you?'

'No, of course not, Mother!' Cara almost choked

with indignation. 'How could you even think such a thing!'

'I merely wondered, that's all,' Lilian appeased her, her hands fluttering from this to that on the dressing-table without actually touching anything. 'I believe his sister will be coming up from Johannesburg for the wedding this afternoon.'

'So Vince told me,' Cara confirmed, still finding it difficult to use his name, and suppressing a shiver at the thought of what still lay ahead of her.

'She's a doctor, I think he said, and she isn't married.'

'That's correct.'

'Cara. . . .' Those slender, fluttering hands gripped Cara's arms with surprising strength. 'Are you absolutely sure that this is what you want?'

No, God help me, this isn't what I want! Cara bit the words back forcibly as they rose to her lips, and she swallowed down the growing lump of fear in her throat. For her mother's sake she had to remain silent. Her father knew the truth, and it was bad enough having to watch him suffer.

'Yes, Mother, I'm sure,' Cara heard herself saying in an admirably calm voice as she met her mother's eyes on a level with her own. 'Now, please go downstairs and keep Dad company while I do my make-up . . . and stop worrying.'

'How can I stop worrying,' Lilian wailed. 'You're my only daughter, and I care about you, and . . . oh, I'd better take a handkerchief because I know I'm going to cry.'

Lilian Lloyd hurried out of the room and closed the door, but she left behind a hint of her delicate, fragrant perfume. The familiarity of it brought the sting of tears to Cara's eyes, but she controlled herself with a formidable effort and studied herself absently in the mirror.

Her lustrous dark hair was coiled into a knot in the nape of her neck, and a tortoise-shell comb held it firmly in place. Her tawny eyes were fringed with long dark lashes which often hid the sparkle of humour there, but in anger her eyes could become dark and stormy. Cara had been blessed with an even temperament, but during the past few days Vince Steiner had had her fluctuating between a simmering and an explosive anger which she had never known before. It was as if his mere presence triggered off something inside her which inevitably brought out the worst in her. Her peaceful existence had been shattered, and her usually tranquil mind was filled with disturbing, turbulent thoughts.

Cara nervously fingered the modest neckline of her pale jade dress, but when she noticed the tremor in her hand she dropped it to her side at once and curled her fingers into her palm. Her face was pale beneath the tan she had acquired during the recent summer months, and her eyes had become dark pools of naked fear. She looked like someone preparing to go to a funeral instead of a wedding, she realised in a spurt of rational thought, and she began to apply her make-up with precisional care in an attempt to hide what lay beneath.

She would never forget the expression on her father's face three nights ago when, confronted by Vince Steiner in her father's study, she had consented to become Vince's wife. Her father had been torn between a deep concern for her and a guilt-ridden relief, and he had started to shake, his face going a chalk white. Cara had wanted to weep when she had witnessed his agony, but Vince Steiner had been obnoxiously triumphant about his easy victory.

Cara felt a rising hatred at the memory, but her hatred was soon replaced with fear. Within less than two hours she would be married to a man she did not love; a man who seemed to repel her with everything he did and said, and for a year she would have to endure whatever he chose to do to her. Shudder after shudder rippled through her, but she resolutely shut her mind to the thoughts which threatened to create chaos with her outwardly calm, serene appearance. For her father's sake, *and* her mother's, she would have to hide her feelings. During the long hours of the night she had tutored herself into feeling nothing but numb acceptance, and to give way now would be to admit defeat.

She picked up her wide-brimmed hat, the colour of which was a pale jade to match her dress, and she pinned it to her head at an elegant angle which partially shaded her eyes. Her gloves lay on the bed beside her handbag and, when she got up to fetch them, there was a tap on her door.

'Are you ready, Cara?' David Lloyd asked moments later when he stood facing her, and her heart wept for him when she saw the greyness of his pallor.

'Yes, Dad, I'm ready.' But how ready was she? Her mouth felt as dry as dust, and every so often fear would clutch at her insides until her nerves coiled themselves into an aching knot of tension at the prospect of what lay ahead of her.

David Lloyd glanced quickly over his shoulder as if to make sure they were alone, then he stepped farther into the room. 'This is most probably the only moment we will have alone together, and I have so much to say to you.'

'Dad, I——'

'No, no, I must say it,' he interrupted, gripping her cold hands tightly. 'I want you to know that I hate myself for doing this to you. I appreciate the fact that you are marrying Steiner to save my skin, but I shall never forgive myself for allowing you to become involved in this.'

Cara desperately wanted to reassure him, but she knew that if she opened her mouth to speak her tight control would snap, and the possibility of bursting into tears could not be overlooked.

'It's time to go, David,' her mother's voice drifted towards them from the upstairs landing, and the moment passed.

'Coming, Lilian,' her father replied, raising his voice and, linking Cara's arm with his, they walked out of her room.

It was a warm autumn afternoon in the north-eastern Transvaal, but Cara shivered intermittently during the short trip into town. She felt like a condemned prisoner being driven to the gallows and, without thinking, she raised a trembling hand to smooth away that awful tightness about her throat.

The chestnut trees had long since prepared themselves for the coming winter, and their leaves lay scattered like a golden carpet across the streets and pavements of Murrayville. The town had expanded since the first steel plant had been erected. Buildings had risen in the shopping areas almost like mushrooms overnight, and more than two thousand houses had been erected on the south side of the town to accommodate the workers in the factory. The once clear sky was now becoming polluted with smoke spiralling from the tall chimneys, and the older inhabitants were beginning to balk at the word *progress*. The easy pace of life had been accelerated to the point where only the young could cope, and hard-bitten people like Vince Steiner were elected on to committees which dealt solely with modernisation and growth.

Vince Steiner. His name alone struck a chill in Cara's heart. He was a deadly opponent in business, she had been told, and a force to be reckoned with in the various fields of industry where he had a say. He was known for his ruthlessness in getting what he wanted, and he was seldom crossed because of the power he wielded. This was the man she was going to marry, and the mere thought of it was enough to want to make her shrivel up and die.

No one spoke in the car. It was indeed like going to a funeral and, when her father turned into the parking area beside the magistrate's offices, Cara found that she was clenching her hands so tightly in her lap that they actually ached.

Vince appeared as if from nowhere when Cara stepped out of the car into the warm sunshine, and his sister, Harriet, stood beside him. Harriet was tall and slender with short fair hair curling about her face. She was an attractive, strong-featured woman, and the clasp of her hands was firm when Vince introduced them.

Cara tried to relax, but she could not. Vince seemed to loom larger than life beside her, and his big hand beneath her elbow sent a charge of feeling through her which she was too terrified to analyse. His dark grey suit and white shirt was a perfect foil for his tanned complexion and sun-bleached hair, and his ruggedly handsome features frightened rather than pleased her.

'Smile, Cara,' he warned in his deep-throated voice as he drew her a little aside. 'Or am I to believe you want your mother to know that you're marrying me under protest?'

Cara forced a frozen smile to her lips and shivered despite the warmth of the afternoon sun as they walked towards the old stone building. Her personal effects were already in his possession, they had been transferred to his home early that morning, and all that remained now was for Vince Steiner to take legal possession of *her*. She wished that she could start running and never stop, but they were entering the building with her parents, and his sister was following close behind.

Everything had its limits, even fear and tension, Cara discovered when they all crowded into the small, impersonal little room and stood facing the lanky, bearded magistrate. Something died inside her and a blessed numbness took over that carried her through the brief ceremony. She was conscious of the sickly smell of furniture and floor polish while the magistrate's unemotional voice rattled off the necessary words. It was as if she stood outside herself while she voiced the required words at the given moment. A plain gold wedding band was slipped on to her finger. It felt cold and unfamiliar, and from the recesses of her mind a cry exploded. *Too late!*

The wedding ceremony was over, and there was no going back. A strong hand tipped her face up, and cool, very male lips were pressed against hers. She was neither repelled, nor excited by their brief contact. She was, in fact, too numb to feel anything, but she forced herself to smile as she accepted Harriet's cool congratulations, and embraced her tearful mother. She embraced her father as well, and for one brief moment she glimpsed the naked suffering in his eyes before Vince took her firmly by the arm and led the party out of the building. She had signed her name in that impersonal little office for the last time. She was now Mrs Vince Steiner, and there was nothing to rejoice about in this knowledge.

The drive out to his house was accomplished in silence, and Cara was only vaguely aware of the sun-drenched terraced garden surrounding the white-washed house with its colourful awnings at the windows. When they were all assembled in the living-room with its modern furnishings, Cara felt the numbness leave her, and the tension returned with a vengeance that knotted her insides and clutched at her throat as if to strangle her. White-coated black servants carried in an assortment of snacks, and a champagne cork popped prior to the glasses being filled.

Everyone seemed to be talking at the same time; everyone except Cara, that is. She smiled because she knew she had to, but she left it to her father and Vince to carry out the farce verbally. Harriet's pale grey eyes met Cara's a few times, and there was something in their depths that disturbed Cara. How much did Harriet know? Was she aware of the situation, or was she simply curious about her brother's sudden decision to marry a woman she had had no prior knowledge of?

'I'd like to propose a toast,' Vince announced when the late afternoon sun began its swift descent in the west, and a heavy arm was draped about Cara's slim waist to press her against his hard side. The warmth of his hand was burning her through the silk of her dress against her hip, and Cara felt a strange tremor racing through her. Her heart leapt into her throat with a force that made her catch her breath, and she raised her eyes to meet his compelling glance for the first time that day. Her parents and Harriet had ceased their conversation, and during that brief silence Cara felt as if she had become suspended over a deep and dangerous ravine. Vince's eyes held hers captive, the gleam of triumph in their depths changing swiftly to a warning when she made to draw away, and his strongly chiselled mouth curved in a derisive smile as he raised his glass. 'To my beautiful bride.'

The sides of their glasses touched before they raised them to their lips, and when Cara sipped at the sparkling champagne it tasted like vinegar in her mouth.

'I think I'm going to cry,' Lilian wailed, creating a welcome diversion which allowed Cara to draw away from Vince.

'No, you're not,' David Lloyd stated firmly, glancing at his watch. 'Drink your champagne, Lilian, and let's go home.'

Lilian dabbed at her eyes with a lace handkerchief and controlled herself with an obvious effort, but the tears were brimming in her eyes once again when Cara accompanied them out to her father's car a few minutes later.

'Take care of yourself, Cara,' Lilian whispered as they embraced each other.

'I'm not leaving the country, Mother,' Cara reminded her, forcing a laugh along her throat to her lips. 'I'll still be working at the library, and I'll see you often.'

David Lloyd did not say anything, but his eyes spoke volumes when they met Cara's. He kissed her lightly on the cheek and, with one last long look, he got into the BMW beside her mother, and drove away.

The last rays of the sun were warm against Cara's face and arms, but she stood there shivering. She had to go back into the house, and she dreaded it. It was of some consolation to know that Harriet was still there, and this gave Cara the necessary courage to go inside and face them.

The atmosphere seemed vaguely strained when she entered the living-room, and her own tension spiralled to an alarming pitch.

'I think I'd like to freshen up a little,' Cara announced, desperate suddenly to get away from this man she had married, and desperate also to get away from his sister who was eyeing her now with something between hatred and pity.

'Turn to the right upstairs,' Vince directed Cara almost absently. 'Our bedroom is on the left, and you'll find the servants have unpacked your things.'

Our bedroom. The words shot a chill of alarm through Cara, but she thrust it from her, and shut her mind to everything except her immediate desire to be on her own.

'Thank you,' she murmured abruptly, walking quickly out of the living-room, and across the hall.

She ascended the carpeted stairs and turned to the left when she reached the upper floor. Confronted by three doors, she opened the first curiously and found herself in a small bedroom. There was a single bed against the one wall, and a chest of drawers against the other, she discovered. The curtains were drawn across the window, but even in the dimness she could see that the sparsely furnished room was enhanced only by a built-in cupboard with slatted doors. She opened the second door and found herself in a white-tiled bathroom with a green towel draped over the bath rail. The personal toiletries on the shelf belonged to Vince, and she stepped swiftly back into the passage. The third door led into a large bedroom with a window facing the terraced front garden. The curtains at the window were a deep blue to match the quilted bedspread on the enormous double bed with its carved wooden head-board, and the wall-to-wall carpeting was a pale aquamarine in contrast. Here also built-in cupboards with slatted wooden doors lined the length of the one wall, and a dressing-table had been built into it.

Cara pressed a switch on the slab of the built-in dresser, and a tube light lit up the area above the mirror. She stared at herself and she had the curious sensation that she was looking at a stranger. Her facial muscles were so tense that it seemed as if her skin was stretching too tightly across the fine bone structure of her features, and the shadows beneath her eyes were accentuated by the sickly yellow of her complexion.

She took off her hat, and in the mirror she could see the light flashing on the gold of her wedding ring. She felt sick inside as she turned away from that image and, when she flung her hat across the room on to the bed, she tugged the ring off her finger. She stood with that circle of gold between her trembling fingers and knew the desire to fling it from her as well, but she knew such an action would not solve her problem. Whether she wore Vince Steiner's ring, or not, she was legally his wife. *Possession* was a better word, she thought cynically. A mere hour ago she had signed away her independence, and by doing so she had given him a legal right to her body.

Oh, God! She thrust the ring back on to her finger and raised her hands to her throbbing temples. She did not want to think about it, but she could not curb her mind. The mere thought of his hands touching her body made her shudder, and she could only hope that he would give her a little time to adapt to the situation before he claimed her totally.

Her palms felt damp and, thrusting aside her thoughts, she opened the door leading out of the bedroom, and walked into a bathroom so large one could almost lose oneself in it. She washed her hands in the basin and dried them on the spotlessly white towel. Her vanity case containing her make-up and toiletries had somehow found its way from her father's car into the bathroom, and she hastily powdered her nose and touched up her lipstick. She looked a little better even though she did not feel any better, and a few minutes later she was making her dreaded way down the stairs.

'I know and I can understand your desire for vengeance, but you're taking things too far, Vince.'

Harriet's clear, precise voice reached Cara's ears when she was halfway down the last flight of stairs, and the word 'vengeance' made her freeze on the spot.

'I'll do as I see fit,' Vince's harsh voice replied while Cara was still trying to decide whether she had heard Harriet correctly.

'You've never taken advice from anyone, and I know you won't take mine, but I can't pretend that I condone your marriage to Cara Lloyd.'

'She is Cara Steiner now,' he reminded his sister with a bitter, stinging sarcasm that made Cara wince inwardly for some reason. 'By taking David Lloyd's daughter, my dear Harriet, I'm hitting him where it hurts most, and that is exactly what I've been waiting for all these years.'

Cara's hand tightened in pain and confusion on the wooden balustrade until her knuckles whitened. What was Vince and his sister talking about? What need was there for vengeance when he had already extracted the price for his extension of the agreement between him and her father?

'Sometimes, Vince, I find you despicable,' Harriet's disapproving voice intruded on Cara's bewildered thoughts. 'You're using her as a pawn in this deadly game of revenge you're playing. The fact that she is innocent, and is probably quite unaware of her father's actions, simply don't count with you. You are going to use her and abuse her before you finally shuttle her back to her father, and in the end you're still going to break David Lloyd for what he did. Doesn't it concern you that you will have ruined her life as well?'

'One man's actions ruined our father's life as well as mine, and what concerns me is that David Lloyd must pay in full for what he did.'

Even at a distance the savage anger in his voice made Cara cringe, but she remained where she was, becoming wiser and also increasingly confused with every second that passed.

'I suffered too, Vince, and don't forget that,' Harriet hit back, 'but I've discovered that taking revenge can never right a wrong. It can only create another wrong which could be a hundred times worse.'

'Philosophically that may be so, but I will at least have the satisfaction of knowing that Lloyd has suffered as much as we did.'

'I don't think I know you anymore,' Harriet broke the brief silence which had followed his remark, and there was now a ring of sadness in her voice. 'You've become hard and callous through the years, and that's not like you at all.'

'Circumstances have made of me what I am, Harriet, and now that I have him where I want him I'm going to carry out the rest of my plans whether you approve or not,' Vince argued harshly. 'He'll pay in full even if it's the last thing I do on this earth.'

'Well, don't expect me to applaud you in the end,' Harriet retorted with a burst of icy anger that matched her brother's, and the next instant she was marching into the hall and slamming the living-room door behind her.

Harriet paused in the centre of the hall at the sight of Cara coming down the stairs, and there was a measure of guilt in her glance as she searched Cara's rigidly controlled features.

'I shan't be joining you for dinner after all,' she announced stiffly when Cara stood facing her.

'Oh,' Cara murmured, taken aback. 'I'm sorry.'

And she *was* sorry. Harriet's presence would have lessened part of the ordeal which still lay ahead of her, but now she would have to see it through on her own.

Harriet turned to leave, but at the door she paused again and glanced back over her shoulder with a grim expression on her face. 'I want you to know that I don't approve of what my brother has done, and I would have prevented this marriage if I could have done so.'

Cara stared at her, searching for the right words, but finding none. Harriet most probably hated her as much as Vince, but there had been a hint of humanity in her remark, and a little warmth stole into Cara's body for the first time that day.

'Thank you for telling me how you feel,' she said at length, and Harriet looked at her strangely for a moment before she nodded abruptly and walked out of the house to where she had parked her car.

Cara braced herself to face Vince alone, and she opened the door of the living-room to find him standing in front of the stone fireplace. He had been staring broodingly into the empty grate, but he looked up when she entered and fixed his cold eyes dispassionately on her person.

'More champagne?' he asked abruptly, gesturing towards the bottle which was still quite full, but she shook her head.

'No, thank you.'

'Harriet has left.'

'Yes, I know.' She bit down hard on her lip to steady it. 'I met her in the hall just as she was leaving, and she explained.'

His eyes narrowed almost imperceptibly. 'What did she explain?'

This was not the moment to confront him with what

she had overheard. It was all still too puzzling to
comprehend fully, and she doubted also whether she
would hear the complete truth from Vince. He seemed
to imagine that her father had done something terrible
and, not knowing what it was, she was not in a position
to defend her father. She would have to be patient if she
was to learn the truth, because Vince Steiner was not a
man to be questioned, and she would have to wait until
he was in a tolerant mood.

'Harriet doesn't approve of our marriage,' she said
instead, and he snorted disparagingly.

'Being a doctor has made her soft in the head.'

'Being a doctor has probably made her more aware
of human frailties,' she contradicted, and a look of
scorn flashed across his face.

'What she doesn't realise, Cara, is that there are
some things which cannot be left unpunished,' he said
through clenched teeth, and his remark would have
been totally confusing if she had not heard the
conversation between him and his sister. He snapped on
a light when the darkness of dusk settled in the room,
and when a white-coated servant appeared silently at
the door, he said abruptly: 'Let's go and have dinner.'

They sat facing each other across the extremities of
an oval table. Neither of them spoke unless they were
forced to, and they went from the consommé through
to the sweet without Cara actually knowing what she
had eaten, or whether she had eaten at all. She still had
that hollow feeling at the pit of her stomach when their
coffee was served in the living-room, and although she
avoided looking directly at Vince, she was aware of his
presence with every fibre of her tense, quivering being.
He was watching her, and she knew it. His eyes
followed every movement she made like a predatory
animal observing its prey, and her frantic mind

wondered if he was trying to decide on the right moment to pounce, but he made no such attempt while they drank their coffee.

He lit a cigarette and stretched himself out in his chair. He looked so perfectly calm and relaxed that she hated him for the way she felt. The clock on the mantelshelf struck the hour, jarring her nerves, and she was surprised to see that it was only eight o'clock. The tensions of the day had piled up inside her to leave her exhausted, and there was nothing she longed for more than to put her head down somewhere to sleep away the fears which had haunted her the past twenty-four hours.

'You're not very talkative, are you,' Vince broke the silence between them, and the sound of his deep-throated voice brushed gratingly across the ends of her raw nerves. 'You have hardly said a word since we sat down to dinner.'

'I wasn't aware that you wanted to make conversation,' she excused herself coolly.

'It seems I've married a phenomenon,' he remarked scathingly. 'A woman who doesn't tire a man out with her senseless chatter is quite rare.'

She felt inexplicably hurt, and she put down her cup to clasp her hands tightly in her lap. 'Your sarcasm is uncalled for.'

'You misunderstand, Cara,' he mocked her, and his narrowed, sometimes lazy eyes slid from hers to where the silk of her dress clung softly to the curve of her breasts. 'I was complimenting you.'

'Really?' she said icily, trying to ignore that hated sensation that she had been touched physically by his eyes as they roamed over her body, and his soft, throaty laughter made her suspect that he was aware of every spark of feeling he aroused in her.

'I can sense that you want to start an argument, my dear, and I refuse to argue with you on our wedding night.'

Wedding night! The words conjured up in her mind those passionately tender moments which a bride would spend in the arms of the man she loved, but for Cara her wedding night was simply a nightmare yet to come. She shut her mind to those thoughts, but she could not shut out the anger which had risen at the thought of what she would be denied.

'It was a ghastly wedding,' the words were torn from her before she could prevent them, and she cursed herself when she saw him eyeing her with speculative mockery.

'Would you have preferred something more spectacular in a church?'

'No, I wouldn't have, and you know it!' she retorted angrily. 'Our marriage is a farce, and if it had taken place in a church I would have been forced to make vows before God which I know very well I shan't be keeping.'

'You're tense and overwrought, Cara,' he smiled, but his eyes were like cold bits of steel raking her. 'I suggest you go up to bed, and I'll have a whisky before I do the same.'

Cara could think of nothing else at that moment except that it would be a relief to get away from him, and she fled from the living-room without waiting for a second invitation.

She was panting when she reached the bedroom, and only then did his words hit home to her. He had said that he would have a whisky before he went to bed. Which bed? The one across the passage in the single room, or this one? Oh, God, she had to stop torturing herself in this way! It was all so unnecessary . . . wasn't it?

Cara took a leisurely bath in an attempt to relax, but the tension in her muscles did not ease entirely, and she was still considerably tense when she stepped out of the bath and dried herself. The nightgown she pulled on was one her mother had given her for her twenty-fourth birthday a month ago, and when she returned to the bedroom she pulled the tortoise-shell comb from her hair to release it from its confining coil. It cascaded down on to her shoulders, heavy and lustrous, and she brushed it vigorously until it was a glossy, silky mass about her face. She flicked her hair back over her shoulders and reached for her jar of night cream, but at that moment there was a knock on the door that made her leap across the room to where she had left her robe on the bed.

The door opened before she could enquire who it was, and she barely had time to clutch the robe like a shield against her body before she found herself facing Vince across the room. He must have downed his whisky in haste, and the dampness of his hair indicated that he had showered in the bathroom across the passage. A brown towelling robe reached down to above his knees, displaying muscled calves. He had nothing on his feet, and when she raised her glance she found herself looking into steel-grey eyes which were observing her with equal intensity. Panic rose within her, but she forced herself to remain outwardly calm.

'What do you want?' she asked when he closed the door and approached her, and still she would not believe what was now becoming the obvious, glaring truth.

Vince thrust his hands into the pockets of his robe, and he paused barely a pace away from her to survey her with a sardonic gleam in his eyes. He was so tall that she had to tilt her head several inches to look up at him, and a frightened pulse was beginning to drum wildly at the base of her throat.

'What do I want?' he repeated her query with a derisive smile. 'Now is that a question for a wife to ask her husband on their wedding night?'

CHAPTER THREE

THE moment Cara had dreaded most was no longer something she could cast aside in her thoughts. She had known deep down that Vince was not going to spare her, but she had foolishly imagined that a spark of humanity lurked somewhere behind that harsh, unrelenting exterior. She realised now, of course, that he did not possess one humane particle in his entire body. Or was his threatening attitude part of that revenge he had spoken of to Harriet?

Cara felt more than threatened; she felt terrified. The only light she had switched on in the room was the one on the bedside cupboard, and quite suddenly the room seemed to be filled with sinister shadows that made her shiver.

'You don't—you can't really mean to—to——'

'To what, Cara?' Vince demanded when she faltered helplessly, and the harshness in his voice sent a renewed shiver of fear racing through her. 'Say it!'

He knew exactly what she had intended to say, but it was obvious that hearing her put her fears into words would afford him a satanic pleasure, and Cara was too afraid at that moment to deny him that enjoyment.

'You can't mean to—to make love to me?' her voice cracked nervously on those revealing words.

'You may rest assured, Cara, that *love* will not enter into our relationship.' He looked for a moment as if he had been chiselled out of pure granite, and the only thing alive about him seemed to be his eyes. They glittered with a strange fire as they flicked over her smooth shoulders which were bare except for, the narrow lacy straps of her nightgown, and her knuckles whitened as her hands tightened defensively on the robe she clutched against her. 'What I intend doing tonight is to take possession of the security your father has given me in lieu of his loan,' he added with cold deliberation.

Her heart was pumping ice into her veins with every thudding beat, and she started to shake uncontrollably. 'To take a woman in cold blood is the most despicable thing a man could do, and I would never have believed that you could stoop so low, but I should have known you would act in this loathsome way.'

He smiled as she imagined the devil might smile in a moment of triumph and, when he raised his hands to caress her bare shoulders, it felt as if the fires of hell were licking against her skin. 'You may insult me as much as you wish, but it will not alter the situation.'

'Please be reasonable,' she pleaded, injecting a forced calmness into her voice which she prayed would deter him, but when she would have moved away from him his hands tightened on her shoulders in a bone-crushing grip.

'I consider that I have been most reasonable, and you can't say that I left you in any doubt as to what I wanted,' he announced harshly and, as a drowning man might see his past life unfold before him, Cara saw her fate in Vince's glittering eyes seconds before he jerked the robe from her hands and flung it across the room.

She stood between him and the light, and his eyes burned down the length of her as he surveyed her body through the revealing material. Hot with embarrassment she tried to pull away from him, but his arm snaked about her waist to crush her softness against his hard length. His free hand wound itself into her hair, and forced her head back until it felt as if her neck would snap. She struggled against him, her clenched fists beating against his chest, but there was no escape from the brute strength of his arms, and his soft, throaty laughter mocked her puny efforts as he lowered his head to claim her lips.

Her head was spinning, and a wave of helplessness surged through her that brought on a faintness, but she fought against the darkness that threatened to envelop her. His mouth was clamped on hers with a force that parted her lips, and the shiver of unwanted emotion that raced through her made her renew her attempt to escape from him. Using her hands as leverage, she tried desperately to push him away from her, but his robe had parted in the struggle, and her hands encountered the roughness of chest hair and warm skin. Her touch aroused his desire, and she could feel it in the tautness of his body against hers, and fear made her fight like a wildcat lashing out for survival.

Vince's hand tightened painfully in her hair, making her cry out, and his mouth left hers to rake fire along her throat and across her shoulder.

'For pity's sake ... please ... let me go!' Her voice was halting and choked with terror, but the only answer she received was the decisive snap of those fragile straps across her shoulders, and the flimsy garment slithered down her shivering body.

He laughed down into her flaming face as he lifted her in his hard arms and carried her towards the bed, and she fought against him, legs and arms flailing, but her blows made no impact on him. She was almost flung on to the bed, and she tried to roll away from him towards the other side, but he held her down effortlessly with one hand while with the other he removed his robe.

Cara's breath was rasping in her throat, and she was

staring a little wildly at his magnificent physique with the wide shoulders tapering down to lean hips. His naked maleness was almost too overwhelming to cope with at that precise moment, and she fought like a demon when he finally pinned her body to the bed with the weight of his own. The heat of his flesh against her own did something to her that she refused to acknowledge, and sheer terror began to dictate her words and her actions.

'You're a cold-blooded, callous, sadistic beast!' she screamed, her nails raking across his shoulders and drawing blood on the muscled flesh.

He drew back momentarily in pain and hissed, 'You will pay for that!'

That was no idle threat, Cara discovered, and she paid for her actions in a most diabolical and unexpected way. One hand was sufficient to pin her arms above her head, and his heavy thigh was flung across hers to imprison her while his free hand indulged in a sensual exploration of her body. Her mind rejected what he was doing to her, but her body responded with a will of its own, and in that way she paid more dearly than if he had struck her physically. She had imagined that the touch of his hands on her body would make her shudder with revulsion, but instead his trailing fingers were kindling a fire in her which she was incapable of dousing. His hand cupped the swell of her breast, his thumb moving back and forth across the hardened peak, and she could not suppress the moan of pleasure that burst from her lips when his warm, moist mouth followed suit.

This man was not a cold-blooded, callous, sadistic beast as she had berated him. He was an expert lover who knew exactly how to please a woman, and it was this discovery that started a rebellion in Cara. A part of her wanted to surrender to the feelings he was arousing, but a part of her also rejected it. There was no love involved, and if she allowed him access to her body it would be nothing but *lust*. Her mind was still rational enough to find the word abhorrent. It was wrong to feel this way about a man she did not love; it was loathsome and degrading, and her body writhed beneath him in protest.

'Stop behaving like a damn virgin!' he growled against her breast when she had freed her hands and was clawing at him in an attempt to escape.

'But I *am* a virgin!' she cried out in anger and growing despair, and his hands stilled its caress along her thigh as his head shot up to look down into her tear-filled eyes.

'Well, what do you know,' he mocked her ruthlessly. 'So I have indeed taken Lloyd's most prized possession.'

His sobering words dried her tears, forcing her to recall Harriet's accusation that he would use her like a pawn in this game of vengeance only to shuttle her back to her father when he had reached his goal, and the look in his eyes told her that this was exactly what she was. She was a pawn in this dirty game of revenge, and the realisation sent a stab of pain through her which she could not understand at that moment.

'I hate you, Vince Steiner!' she hissed with a ferocity which was alien to her nature. 'I hate you, do you hear!'

'Hate me as much as you want, Cara,' he laughed that triumphant laugh of the devil. 'Hate puts fire in your veins, and I prefer my women fiery rather than meek.'

'You're disgusting!' she spat out the words, but he was unperturbed by her insult.

'You're beautiful when you're angry, Cara, and I

would never have believed that your skin could feel like warm silk beneath my hands,' he taunted her while his hand boldly explored the feminine contours of her body, and detoured along intimate places. 'You have fought like a tigress, but you have only succeeded in making me want you more, and before I am finished with you I'll have you purring like a kitten in my arms.'

'*No!*' she denied his statement vehemently, but her treacherous body was already responding to the sensual and fiery arousal of his caressing fingers.

'Yes, *liebchen*,' he contradicted throatily, his teeth nibbling playfully at the small lobe of her ear and sending shivers of unwanted pleasure racing through her taut, quivering body. 'Sheath your claws and relax, my little kitten. It is inevitable that you will purr for me before this night is over.'

Cara resisted him in mind if not in body, and the pain of his possession wrenched a cry from her which he stifled with his mouth. She was still hating him for hurting her when the pain receded to make way for a fierce pleasure that shattered all her maidenly illusions. In the final moments she lost complete control, and she was oblivious of the fact that she clung to him as if he were a safety raft in this storm-tossed sea of emotions he had plunged her into. She felt as if he was lifting her out of herself to a realm where nothing existed beyond the exquisite tension gripping her, and she soared on towards that unknown summit until her flight culminated in a rush of explosive sensations so intensely pleasurable that she wanted to die with the sweetness of it.

'*Vince!*' she cried out his name as he sagged on top of her in a shuddering groan, and she hated the thought of what her raggedly revealing voice must have told him.

Their bodies were damp with perspiration, their

hearts thundering in the aftermath of passion and, as sanity returned slowly and painfully, a deep sense of shame washed over Cara. She had not exactly purred as he had predicted, but she had surrendered herself willingly and, no matter how much she tried to deny it, she had enjoyed what he had done to her.

Vince eased his heavy body from hers, but when she would have leapt out of bed his hands reached for her and pulled her back into his arms.

'Liebchen,' he murmured close to her ear, burying his face in her fragrant hair, and the deep timbre of his voice was almost a caress.

'Don't call me that!' she protested sharply.

'Why not?'

'Liebchen means sweetheart, and I'm not your sweetheart!'

She turned her face into the pillow when he raised his head to look at her, but strong fingers gripped her chin, and she was forced to meet the mockery in her eyes. 'After what we have shared I should imagine I am entitled to call you liebchen, don't you think?'

'Why use the German word anyway,' she argued, her cheeks flaming with embarrassment, and then the most extraordinary thing happened.

Vince's face hardened, and he released her at once. He swung his legs off the bed and sat up to reach for his robe on the floor, but, instead of putting it on, he flung it on to the chair in the corner. 'My father was German, didn't you know?'

'No, I didn't,' she confessed quietly, her wary eyes on his broad, muscled back. 'And your mother?'

'My mother was a South African,' he answered abruptly, his hands gripping the side of the bed.

'Why do you speak of them in the past tense?'

The muscles rippled in his back when he moved his

shoulders in something like a careless shrug. 'They are both dead.'

'Oh.' She shivered and pulled the sheet up to cover her body. 'I'm sorry.'

'Are you?' he questioned cynically, turning his head to look at her with shuttered eyes.

'You sounded so bitter,' she explained lamely, wishing suddenly that she had not questioned him about his parents.

'You have said that you hate me, and yet you are concerned that I should sound bitter about the death of my parents.' He shook his head as if in confusion, and eyed her mockingly. 'You surprise me and intrigue me more and more, Cara, *liebchen*.'

Annoyed that he should mock her sincerity, she turned sharply on to her side so that she faced away from him. 'I am not insensitive to the things which hurt people, and hating you doesn't change that.'

'They say hatred is akin to love, Cara. Take care that you don't love me, *liebchen*, because that will never do.'

'I could never love you,' she spat out the words as she sat up to face him furiously. 'You are everything that I despise in a man, and you might as well know it. No honourable man would have forced a woman into a marriage she did not want, and no man with a sense of decency would have done what you did to me tonight.'

Their eyes locked for several electrifying seconds. She was alarmingly certain she had gone too far, but he turned towards her with apparent calmness, and leaned over her in a way that made her draw a quick nervous breath as she fell back against the pillows. The width of his shoulders blotted out the light, but she was being scorched and blinded by that devilish gleam in his eyes, and she wished suddenly that she had had the sense to keep her mouth shut.

'It was inevitable that I should hurt you a little,' he mocked her, 'but it was not so terrible in the end, was it?'

Her body still tingled with the memory of his caresses, and her colour deepened at the mere thought of the intimacies they had shared. She tried to sustain his probing glance, but fear of what he might see made her lower her eyes hastily to his wide chest where the short, golden hair curled tightly against his deeply tanned skin. Vince was not a callow youth she could deceive with a denial. He was an experienced lover who must have known women intimately, and he was fully aware of how she had reacted physically. He was determined to make her admit the pleasure he had given her, but she was equally determined not to give him that satisfaction even though he was aware of the truth. He was using her to hurt her father, and she had to remember that.

'You're a man of experience so I will not account for my physical response, but mentally I hated every moment of it,' she cried with a fierceness which was aroused out of loyalty to her father, and her anger increased when Vince's silent laughter shook the bed. 'Don't laugh, because I mean it!'

'Yes, Cara, I am sure you mean it,' he mocked her and, flicking the switch of the bedside light, he plunged the room into darkness 'Goodnight, *liebchen.*'

'Goodnight.' Her lips felt stiff, and her body was quiveringly taut when she felt him slide between the sheets. 'And don't call me *liebchen*,' she added coldly.

Vince did not reply, and moments later his shallow, deep breathing told her that he was asleep. It was incredible! Her anger alone had robbed her of the desire to sleep, but it was obvious that nothing prevented Vince from going to sleep when he wished to do so.

Cara lay awake wrestling with her thoughts for some time, and there was also the unfamiliarity of sleeping with a man in the bed beside her. Fear had kept her awake the night before, but this time it was anger and several other things which she would not even admit to herself. Exhaustion finally claimed her, and she slept as if she had taken a sleeping draught.

At one time during the night she had surfaced from her deep sleep to find herself lying in Vince's arms with her head pillowed on his shoulder. Their bodies were close and their legs entwined, but she was asleep again before she could devise a plan to move away from him without waking him.

Something woke Cara on the Sunday morning; a sound perhaps, and she opened her eyes to find the sun streaming into the bedroom through the lace curtains at the window. She was momentarily confused by the unfamilarity of her surroundings, but reality was thrust upon her at the sight of Vince placing a tray on the bedside cupboard next to her. The material of his brown slacks pulled tautly across his muscular thighs, and a shirt of a matching colour was unbuttoned at the collar to expose his strong throat. She had noticed the previous night that his fair, sun-bleached hair had a tendency to curl, but this morning it was brushed back severely to accentuate the broadness of his forehead.

'Good morning, Cara,' he broke the silence between them, his thumbs hooked into the wide snake-skin belt hugging his hips, and his eyes flicking over her with keen interest. 'You have beautiful breasts, *liebchen*, and they are a temptation to get back into bed with you.'

Only then did Cara realise that the sheet had slipped down to her waist, and her cheeks flamed with embarrassment as she hastily pulled the sheet up to below her chin.

'You're hateful!' she accused, flashing him a dark, angry glance, but the mockery in his eyes told her that her anger had left him untouched.

He walked a few paces away to pick up her robe, and he flung it on to the bed within her reach. 'Put this on, and have your breakfast.'

She pulled her robe towards her and knew that there was no way she could put it on without exposing herself yet again. She knew instinctively that Vince would not turn his back on her, and any further display of modesty would simply evoke his hateful mockery, so she grit her teeth and allowed the sheet to fall to her waist while she quickly slipped her arms into the sleeves of her robe. She pulled it about her without bothering to fasten the belt, and she kept the lower half of her body covered with the sheet.

'Why am I being treated to such luxury?' she asked suspiciously, his aftershave lotion quivering in her nostrils when he placed the tray on her knees.

'Let's say I am in a generous mood this morning,' he smiled faintly, but the smile was gone almost before she had time to appreciate it. 'Have your breakfast and get dressed. I have something I want to show you.'

He walked out of the room and, despite his size, his movements were lithe like an athlete. When the door closed behind him her mind conjured up a vision of his naked, muscular body as she had seen it the night before. There was not an ounce of superfluous flesh on his superbly proportioned frame, and the muscles she had seen rippling beneath his skin had indicated a physical fitness which she was certain did not come solely from hours spent in a gymnasium.

She thrust aside Vince's overpowering image of raw masculinity, and lifted the silver lid off the oval platter to discover that he had brought her bacon and eggs and

two slices of toast with coffee. It was almost a
nauseating sight for Cara who seldom had more than a
cup of coffee for breakfast, but something warned her
she might be heading for trouble if she did not at least
make an attempt to eat the meal he had brought up to
her.

Fifteen minutes later Cara could scarcely credit
herself with what she had accomplished. She had
emptied her plate, and she was having her second slice
of toast with her coffee. She could not recall at first
when was the last time she had had a decent meal, and
then she remembered. She had scarcely touched her
food the night before her wedding, and she had had no
more than a cup of coffee for breakfast the previous
morning. For lunch she had taken a bite out of a
sandwich, and last night she had spent her time
rearranging the food on her plate rather than eating it.
Taking everything into consideration, it was no wonder
she had eaten so much this morning.

Cara leapt out of bed when she had finished her
coffee, and dashed into the bathroom. She did not
know Vince very well, but somehow he had not given
her the impression that he enjoyed being kept waiting,
and she wasted no time bathing and changing into
beige slacks and an emerald green blouse with wide
sleeves which were gathered into a lacy frill at the cuff.
She pushed her feet into a pair of green sandals to
match her blouse, and she coiled her hair into its
familiar knot before she applied a little make-up to her
face.

She studied herself critically when she had put on her
lipstick, and she noticed first of all that the paleness of
the day before had gone. She was not quite sure what
she was looking for. Was she expecting to find some
tell-tale sign of what had occurred between Vince and

herself the previous night? The memory of the passion he had aroused in her made her blush like a teenager, but other than that she looked the same. She felt different, though. Maturer? Wiser? She could not say. At twenty-four she had not been totally ignorant of the sexaul functions of the male and female body, but to actually experience such a physical union was a different matter completely to merely reading about it in books. She had never dreamed it could involve so much, and Vince had not been a very tender, loving teacher. He had been demanding in his desire for her, and near brutal in his possession. The flame of his passion had kindled an answering flame in her, and together they had fanned that flame into a roaring inferno.

Together. She shrank inwardly from the word, but she could not deny to herself that she had been aroused sufficiently to become a very willing participant.

Her face was hot, and her body was trembling with the memory of what had occurred, but Vince was waiting for her downstairs, and it took a gigantic effort to control herself to some degree before she could go down and face him.

'Who does this farm belong to?' Cara asked an hour later when Vince's white Mercedes was bounding and swaying along the uneven track between a ploughed field, and a grazing camp which was stocked with cattle.

'It belongs to me,' Vince surprised her. 'I naturally have a manager living on the premises to take care of everything.'

The road forked ahead of them and Vince took the one towards the right to where the trees grew densely along the river's edge. A cottage, newly built out of local stone, nestled amongst the trees close to the river, and Vince parked his car beneath the shelter against the side of the building.

It seemed unlikely to Cara that Vince would have installed a manager in a cottage of such small proportions, so she could only surmise that the cottage was Vince's private retreat, and her suspicions were confirmed when he produced a key and unlocked the door. The interior was small, but sufficient for the needs of one or two people, and it had been very simply built. Everything led off the lounge; the bedroom, the bathroom, and the kitchen. The thick carpet on the floor, and the heavy floral curtains at the window were obviously new, but the furniture was dated. It looked as if Vince had picked up the various pieces at random and had had them renovated, but they were set out attractively around a stone fireplace.

Cara did not venture into the bedroom on her own, but she followed Vince into the tiny kitchen where a small table and two chairs had been thrust up against the one wall to allow for more space.

'Why have you brought me here?' she questioned Vince when her curiosity finally got the better of her.

'I had this little cottage erected some years ago, and this is where I stay when I need to escape from the big bad world of high-power business,' he explained mockingly, drawing the curtains aside at the window to let the sunlight in, and glancing at her briefly. 'Do you like it?'

'Am I supposed to?' she evaded his query antagonistically, and Vince turned away from her with a shrug to fill the kettle from the tap.

'Coffee?'

'Yes, please,' she replied automatically, glancing about her with veiled interest while Vince lit the gas stove and placed the kettle on it to boil. Not for anything in the world was she going to let him guess that there was something about this cottage which had attracted her from the moment she had seen it. 'Does Chantal Webber like this cottage?'

She was incredulous at her own temerity, and it looked for a moment as if her knowledge of Chantal's existence surprised him, but his surprise swiftly made way for stinging mockery. 'She adores it.'

'Has she been here often?' Cara wished she could explain to herself why she was asking questions about something which was actually no concern of hers.

'A couple of times,' Vince replied, leaning his hip against the cupboard and folding his arms across his wide chest so that his shirt pulled tightly across his shoulders. His stance was vaguely threatening, and his icy grey eyes told her she was venturing into forbidden territory, but there was something else she simply had to know.

'Did you explain to her about our marriage.'

'I don't have to account to anyone for my actions, *liebchen*,' he smiled mockingly.

'In other words, she doesn't know you're married to me,' she concluded from his remark, and for seemingly interminable seconds only the hiss of the gas stove could be heard.

'Why are you so concerned about someone you don't even know?' Vince questioned her with a hint of incredulity.

'Ever since you came to Murrayville everyone has known that Chantal Webber is your . . .' she faltered on her ill-chosen words when she looked up into eyes glittering like cold, hard steel.

'My what?' he prompted in an ominously quiet voice, and she felt a little sick inside when she realised that she had gone too far to turn back now.

'Your mistress, I imagine,' she gestured vaguely with her hands in an attempt at casualness before she turned from the stabbing scrutiny of his glance.

'Does that bother you?'

'No, of course not!' she answered coolly. 'I simply wouldn't want her to pounce on me and accuse me of stealing you away from her.'

That was clever, she decided in retrospect when she considered her hastily contrived excuse for her curiosity, but when she happened to glance at Vince she was not so sure that she had convinced him. His derisive smile made her heart bounce uncomfortably, and she cursed herself for that tell-tale warmth invading her cheeks.

'Chantal is a woman of the world, and she is very broad-minded,' he explained, turning his back on her to set out two coffee mugs and to remove the kettle from the stove when the water boiled.

The hiss of gas was silenced when he turned the switch, and Cara found herself staring incredulously at his broad back. 'Do you mean that when our marriage is over you will continue your relationship with her, and she will take you back without condemning you?'

'Exactly.'

'She must be a woman in a million.'

'She is,' Vince replied in his deep, abrupt voice, and Cara wondered at the stab of pain that tore through her as she pushed a mug along the cupboard towards her. 'Drink your coffee and then we will go for a walk.'

The hot liquid scalded her throat and brought tears to her eyes which she blinked away rapidly. They sat down in silence, but it was a silence she was becoming accustomed to. Vince's granite-hard expression gave away none of his thoughts, and she wished that she knew more about this man who had forced her into this unwanted marriage. He had a strong profile with the high-bridged nose, and square, jutting jaw. His features were rugged rather than good-looking, and this was what women found so appealing about him. He had nice hands, Cara admitted to herself, but she winced inwardly at the memory of their punishing strength.

Cara's thoughts became confused at this point. She had told herself that his touch would fill her with a shuddering revulsion, and yet he had aroused shudders of incredible pleasure. His cruel domination of her father had repelled her, but she had to admit there was something about Vince that drew her to him despite everything he had done. She ought to hate him, but she could not conjure up one fragment of hatred at that moment.

Her mind wandered beyond the immediate past, and she paused for the first time to analyse her feelings. She had lived a perfectly normal, tranquil life until Vince had appeared on the scene a year ago, and from that moment she had been both fascinated and wary of the powerful magnetism he exuded. His mere presence in a room had aroused feelings quite alien to her, and she had shied from it in something close to shame. She had resented his blatantly sexual appraisal of her, and her resentment had become magnified when he had threatened her father and herself into complying with his demands.

Resentment. That was what she had felt last night as opposed to revulsion. She had resented the circumstances which had made of her merely an object of Vince's passion, and she had resented the fact that he was capable of arousing such a frightening response in her.

Cara jumped nervously when he thumped his empty mug on to the table, and she hastily swallowed down the last mouthful of coffee when he rose to his feet. His towering frame beside her made her feel threatened and intimidated simultaneously, and she got to her feet hastily to lessen that awe-inspiring feeling.

It took no more than three minutes to reach the river that followed a lazy path down to the ocean, and they walked some distance along the crest of the high, slanted embankment. It was a perfect day for being out in the country. The sun was warm on her skin, but there was a faint chill in the air that did not let her forget it was mid April. Leaves and twigs lay at their feet as if nature had spread out a carpet for them to walk on, and within a month the trees would be totally defrocked of their finery to face the winter with a bareness that made Cara shiver in sympathy.

'Why did you bring me here?' she asked again when they had walked for some distance in silence, and Vince paused in his stride to look out across the river with his thumbs hooked into the snake-skin belt about his waist.

'Does the peace and tranquillity not do something to you, Cara?' he answered her query with another when he finally turned his head to meet her upturned, impatient gaze.

'It does,' she confessed with a fiendish desire to shake him out of his arrogant, self-satisfied shell. 'It makes me realise that I would have enjoyed this day a great deal more with someone of my own choice.'

'Such as?' he demanded harshly, his eyes piercingly bright when they raked her insolently from head to foot. 'Name one man who hasn't been frightened off by your cold, haughty manner?'

'There's John Curtis, for instance,' she countered without hesitation, her mind conjuring up a vision of the lean, dark-haired young man who had been her friend and companion so often during the past years.

'John Curtis!' Vince repeated the name with a harsh bark of laughter which was tainted with cynicism. 'He's just a hungry puppy begging at your table for crumbs.

You slap him down, but he always comes back begging
for more.'

Shock vibrated through her at his scornful and
inaccurate summing up of her relationship with John.
'It's not like that at all. We have been good friends
since the days we were at school together, and we enjoy
each other's company, but there's nothing more to it
than that.'

'You're your father's daughter, Cara,' he accused
with a savage note in his voice that made her back an
involuntary pace away from him. 'You're blind to
everything except that which you want to see. You will
use people for as long as it suits you, but you will drop
them flat the moment the tables are turned and they
happen to need something from you.'

Cara felt a coldness invade her body which had
nothing whatsoever to do with the weather. She could
protect herself against the coldness of the weather, but
she could not protect herself against such an icy
accusation when she had no idea where it had
originated. She was fighting an unfair battle, but she
was not going to give in to that feeling of helplessness.
Something was being withheld from her; something her
father had done, and the unfairness of it was that she
was being punished for it along with her father.

CHAPTER FOUR

'My father is not like that, and neither am I,' Cara felt compelled to protest vehemently as she fought against the hurt inflicted by his accusation. 'We do not use people, and then turn our backs on them when they need us.'

'We'll forget about your father for the moment, but why is it you haven't noticed the way Johnny-boy moons over you?' Vince's lips pulled away from his teeth in a mockingly derisive smile that made her palm itch with the desire to slap his face. 'Good God, the fellow almost swoons at your feet every time you subject him to one of your cool and distant smiles.'

Cara began to shake with suppressed fury, and she clenched her hands at her sides for fear of lashing out at him. 'You don't know what you're talking about, and how dare you stand there and pass judgment when you don't know John and you most certainly don't know me well enough to do so!'

'I know you better than you imagine, *liebchen*,' he corrected smoothly, and she was not deaf to the undercurrent of sensuality in his deep-throated voice. 'I have amused myself for months with the task of observing you, and last night I was rewarded with the discovery that there is a fire simmering beneath that cool exterior you display to the world.' He flicked a lazy finger across her cheek, and smiled mockingly down into her eyes. 'It pleases me to know that I can look forward to a year of spending the most enjoyable nights in bed with you.'

Her cheeks flamed with anger as she backed away from his touch. 'You're the most disgusting man I ... *oh!*'

The heel of her sandal twisted beneath her when she stepped on the protuding root of a tree, and she lost her balance. It all happened so fast that there was no time to grasp at something to break her fall, and she went down heavily to slither down the slanted embankment into the river. The shock of the icy water made her catch her breath on a rasping note a mere fraction of a second before she was completely submerged and, when she surfaced from the murky depths, she found Vince standing at the water's edge with his hands on his hips, and a wide smile curving his mouth.

'If you had wanted to indulge in a swim, Cara, I would have suggested you remove your clothes first,' he mocked her as she got to her feet and waded out unsteadily, and the iciness of the water had not cooled the fire of her anger one iota.

'Oh, you—you——' Her teeth began to chatter, forcing her to relinquish the effort of flinging at him a suitable word to describe exactly what she thought of him.

'Come, let me help you,' he offered, laughing in his voice as he held out his hand invitingly towards her, but her laughter simply infuriated her more.

'Don't touch me!' she hissed through her clenched teeth, waving his hand away. 'Just don't touch me!'

Vince's expression hardened, but he shrugged indifferently and turned away. 'Certainly, if you feel that way about it.'

Cara's sandals were ruined, and her wet clothes were clinging to her body like a second skin. Her hair had come undone to hang limp and cold between her shoulder blades, and she could not remember when, if ever, she had felt this cold before. She had to clench her teeth tightly together to stop them from chattering, and she followed Vince up the slippery embankment on all fours. It was all most undignified, and she took off her sandals to walk back to the cottage on bare feet. The sun would not warm her, and the refreshing breeze that stirred in the trees felt as if it was blowing directly off snow-capped mountains.

Cara's angry eyes were on Vince's broad back, her damp lashes caked together like little spikes, and she felt like committing murder when they entered the cottage and he paused in the lounge to glance at her bedraggled form.

'You look rather wet,' he observed blandly, but that hateful mockery lit his eyes and curved his cynical mouth.

'If you say another word, I—I'll throw something at you, I swear it!' Her voice was shaking with fury as she wrapped her arms about her shivering form, and then, to her horror, she burst into tears.

She turned her back on Vince to hide from him the humilating sight of tears rolling down her cheeks, but she could not hide the fact that her shoulders were shaking with cold and silent sobs. This was one of the faults about herself which she hated most, and it was the reason why she always guarded against becoming angry. Anger nearly always drove her to tears, and she had never been more humiliated by it than at this precise moment.

Cara heard a match being struck, and moments later the sound was followed by the crackle of a wood fire in the grate. The smell of wood-smoke drifted towards her as Vince walked out of the lounge and into the bedroom, and she turned cautiously. The leaping flames in the fireplace beckoned with the promise of warmth and, dropping her ruined sandals on the carpeted floor, she crossed the lounge quickly in the hope of ridding herself of this bone-marrow coldness which gripped her.

'Take off your clothes,' Vince ordered when he returned with a blanket to find her huddling in a shivering bundle on the carpet in front of the fire.

'*No!*' she rejected his suggestion stubbornly, but strong hands gripped her arms and jerked her unceremoniously to her feet.

'I don't want you to catch your death, so take your wet clothes off, or I'll take them off for you.'

He towered over her threateningly, his eyes bitingly cold as they stared down into hers, and she knew with a shrinking feeling that he would not hesitate to undress her. She stared at the blanket in his hands and had to admit to herself that it would be a relief to rid herself of her wet, clinging clothes.

She nodded without speaking for fear that her teeth would chatter embarrassingly, and she turned her back on him while she peeled off her clothes. Her hands were shaking so much that she fumbled with the catch of her bra behind her back, and her cheeks flamed when Vince's hands brushed hers aside to undo the catch for her. The lacy garment joined the rest of her things on the floor, and she stood for a moment clothed only in the glow of the fire before Vince draped the blanket about her shivering body.

Cara lowered herself carefully to the carpet, and leaned with her back against the seat of the sofa while she stretched her feet out towards the warmth of the fire. She heard the clink of glass, and then Vince was bending over her again.

'Drink this while I hang your clothes out to dry,' he instructed, and she clutched the blanket about her with one hand while she wriggled the other out between the folds to take the glass from him.

She sniffed at the amber contents and wrinkled her nose. 'It's brandy.'

'Of course it's brandy,' he confessed harshly. 'You're shivering, and the brandy will warm your insides while the fire will do the rest.'

He did not wait to see whether she obeyed him, but stooped without a flicker of embarrassment to pick up her bundle of wet clothing. It was Cara who felt embarrassed at the thought that he was handling those lacy, personal items and, when he strode out of the cottage through the kitchen, she took a hasty sip of brandy to steady herself. She disliked the taste, but when the first mouthful of fiery liquid hit her stomach she felt the benefit of it almost instantly. She drank it slowly, taking a sip every now and then, and the warmth that spread through her insides made her begin to feel more human. She was also feeling a little dizzy, and a strange languour was shifting into her limbs, giving her an odd sense of well-being.

Vince returned a few minutes later with a towel and a brush which he flung on to the seat behind her. He took her by the shoulders and pushed her a little forward so that he could sit on the sofa behind her, and she was beginning to feel too pleasantly warm and drowsy to object when he proceeded to dry her hair with the towel.

Neither of them spoke, but she was aware of his knees jutting out on either side of her, and the firmness of his hands inside the towel while he rubbed her hair dry made her scalp tingle. She felt warm at last, and strangely cosseted. It was a peculiar, but a pleasant sensation when Vince finally threw the towel aside to brush the tangles out of her hair which was still slightly damp. The action did not match the man she imagined him to be, and it shattered her momentarily when she realised fully how little she knew about this man who was her husband.

Vince finally dropped the brush on to the seat beside him, and pushed her forward again so that he could get up, but he did not leave the room. He sat down in the chair facing her to take off his shoes and socks, and he lit a cigarette as he stretched his feet out towards the fire.

'Feeling better?' he asked, his eyes narrowed as he studied her through a cloud of smoke.

'Yes, thank you.' The corners of her mouth lifted in a smile she could not suppress. 'I imagine I got what I deserved. I have insulted you from the moment we arrived here this morning, and I realise now that I provoked you into saying the things you did.'

A gleam of mockery flickered in his eyes. 'Is that an apology, Cara?'

Her smile deepened, and she put down her empty glass to snuggle deeper into the warm blanket. 'Yes, I suppose it is.'

'I didn't need much provocation from you to speak my mind, and I meant every word I said, so don't expect an apology from me.'

'I wasn't hoping for an apology,' she confessed, but inwardly she could still feel the stinging lash of his accusations. An odd little smile was playing about his mouth, and he studied her long and hard until she shifted uncomfortably beneath his gaze. 'Why are you looking at me like that?'

His smile became deeply etched in cynicism. 'I was thinking that you somehow manage to look haughty and beautiful even when you are wrapped in an unattractive blanket.'

The warmth of the fire could not prevent that chilling sensation that gripped her insides at his use of the word *haughty*. ' "Some people are all quality; you would think they were made up of nothing but title and genealogy. The stamp of dignity defaces in them the very character of humanity, and transports them to such a degree of haughtiness that they reckon it below themselves to exercise either good-nature or good manners," ' she quoted *L'Estrange* softly, almost absently while she stared into the flames, and when she looked up she found Vince's eyes resting intently on her face. 'I am not like that, Vince,' she defended herself.

' "The dignity of truth is lost with much protesting." '

Her eyes widened in surprise. He had quoted Ben Jonson as if he had been a student of literature, and she stared at him thoughtfully as he put out his cigarette and joined her on the carpet in front of the fire.

'I was not protesting, I was stating a fact, but you are naturally free to believe what you wish,' she answered him, disturbed by his nearness, and intensely aware of his arm resting on the seat behind her shoulders.

'I notice you don't object to being told that you are beautiful.'

'Personally I think my mouth is too wide, and my eyes too far apart, but what woman in her right mind would object to being told she is beautiful?'

Her eyes were sparkling with irrepressible humour when she turned her head to glance up at him, but she regretted her action almost instantly. His face was mere inches from her own, and the moment their glances locked she found that she could not look away. His eyes fascinated her. They could change from icy grey to warm blue with his emotions, but at that moment his pupils were so enlarged that his eyes were almost black.

Her heart began to hammer against her ribs, and a nervous tremor raced through her body.

'Your hair is almost dry.' His deep voice soothed and caressed her frayed nerves, and he pushed his fingers through her heavy mass of dark, unruly curls until her scalp tingled with his touch.

A lazy finger traced a line of fire from her ear down to the hollow at the base of her throat, and his arm tightened about her shoulders. For one fleeting moment she contemplated escape, but his warm breath mingled with hers, and then she was lost.

The sensual pressure of his hard mouth parted her lips, and a new warmth surged through her that left her trembling against him. His kiss was not demanding; it was instead a lingering, tantalising, and intensely exciting exploration of her mouth, and it made her feel as if an intoxicating drug was slowly being injected into her bloodstream. She murmured in protest when he raised his lips from hers to seek out the sensitive hollow behind her ear, and he laughed softly while he trailed a slow, teasing path back to her eager, waiting lips.

He knew exactly what he was doing to her, *damn* him, and he was using every erotic trick he was acquainted with to ensure her capitulation. Cara was aware of this; her mind warned against it, but her body was too busy responding to those fingers trailing from her throat to her smooth shoulder. There was fire in his touch; a fire that kindled an answering fire in her, and perhaps the brandy he had given her was to blame for the fact that she felt too lethargic to protest when his hand dipped down inside the blanket to cup the swell of her breast. His thumb moved in lazy, sensuous circles around the hardened peak until a shudder of desire coursed through her, and her body moved willingly with his when he lowered her into a reclining position on the carpet.

His mouth moved hungrily over hers, drawing on the sweetness within before he eased himself away from her. She used this opportunity to regain her breath, and she was only vaguely aware that he was tearing off his shirt with a swiftness that did not give her sufficient time to come to her senses. He was between her and the fire, obliterating its glowing warmth, and she fastened her eyes on to his wide shoulders and hair-roughened chest. He leaned over her, and the clean male smell of him stirred her senses as nothing had ever done before. That aura of raw masculinity which surrounded him made her feel like a fragile piece of china, and her eyes pleaded unconsciously with his for leniency before his mouth swooped down on hers to rekindle the fires he had ignited inside her.

The blanket parted beneath the urgency of his hands, exposing her slender body and shapely legs to his brilliant gaze, and a wave of intense shyness made her turn her face away from him. His laughter mocked her, but there was seduction in the hands that explored her body, and his touch aroused every nerve and sinew to a tingling awareness of that aching void inside her that needed to be filled. A wave of shame engulfed her as her body betrayed her. She tried to thrust Vince from her, but he laughed at her puny efforts and forced his knee between her thighs. The dark curtain of her hair lay spread around her flushed face on the cream-coloured carpet, and he buried his hands in it so that she was forced to meet his probing gaze.

'Don't!' she begged when she saw the naked desire in his eyes, but her plea went unheard.

His lips ravaged hers before trailing a destructive path along the sensitive column of her throat, and a stream of fiery sensations coursed through her body when his mouth began to explore her breast. He was creating exquisite havoc with her emotions, and the intimate arousal of his strong, yet sensitive fingers brought her swiftly to a fever pitch of desire. It was at this crucial point that her mind cruelly underlined the distressing knowledge that she was merely being used.

'Oh, no . . . no!' she moaned breathlessly, her hands flat against his chest in an attempt to push him away from her, but the hair-roughened warmth of his skin against her palms aroused a further spate of unwanted sensation which were beginning to sap her energy.

'Tell me you want me.' His voice was hoarse with unmistakable desire, and there was a stab of fear in the recesses of Cara's mind when she actually found herself on the verge of complying with his wishes.

'No, I won't!' she cried out in protest against his unfair command as well as her own crumbling resistance.

'Say it!' he growled threateningly.

'You—you can't make me—say something I—I don't mean,' she gasped unsteadily, clinging desperately to her pride, but her body was pulsating with a rapidly growing need to be possessed by him.

'You will say it, and you will mean it, because right this minute you want me as badly as I want you,' he murmured savagely against her throat, and she could not deny to herself that this was true.

'Vince, don't—don't make me!' she begged huskily, the erotic urgency of his hands on her burning flesh driving her wild with an intolerable longing that made her want to cry out with agony of it.

Tell me you want me!

His deep-throated instruction seemed to take command of her drugged mind, and her control snapped.

She wanted nothing more at that moment than to surrender herself to him, and her hands moved up around his neck until her fingers locked in the hair at the back of his head.

'Yes, *yes*, I want you!' Her voice was almost unrecognisably husky in submission. 'God help me, but I want you!'

He raised himself away from her, and for one terrifying moment she thought he might find a sadistic pleasure in rejecting her, but instead his hand went to the buckle of his belt to undo it. 'I shall not spare you this time,' he warned darkly as he cast aside his slacks.

Cara would never have believed that making love could be so savage and yet so sweet. In the glowing warmth of the log fire, with the weight of Vince's body grinding her into the carpeted floor, they made love with a ferocious urgency. There was no room for thought in this scaringly passionate fusion of their bodies; Cara was conscious only of the exquisite tension his thrusting body was arousing in her, and she could taste his skin against her wildly seeking mouth. Her actions had become controlled by some hidden instinct she had been unaware of until that moment, and her hands roamed his muscled body with a subconscious eagerness to please. She felt the quivering tension in his large frame, and it gave her a strange feeling to know that she could actually arouse him this way. His murmured words of encouragement educated her as to a man's needs, and she followed where he led, allowing him to take complete control of her.

There had been joy in giving, but afterwards there was also the pain of knowing that Vince had given only with his body. She knew she meant no more to him than any one of those women who had drifted in and out of his life in the past, and she knew also that, in the end, her name would simply be added to that list of women he had known. Cara was, as Harriet had said, no more than a pawn in this devilish game he was playing with her father. It hurt to think about it; it hurt more than she cared to acknowledge, and she did not even want to dwell for a fraction of a second on the reason why she felt this way.

Cara closed her eyes tightly to hold back the sudden rush of tears, and she did not open them when Vince roused himself in silence to put on his clothes. She wrapped the blanket about her naked body, and curled herself up into a tight ball of misery from which she did not stir until she heard Vince walk out of the cottage. His heavy footsteps crunched on the gravel beneath the window, and only when she could no longer hear him did she get up with the blanket still draped about her to go in search of her clothes.

An hour passed, and Vince did not return. Cara considered making something to eat when she found that there was ham and eggs in the gas refrigerator, but she decided against it. Fifteen minutes later she could not tolerate the silence in the cottage a moment longer. The silence seemed threatening somehow and, when she thought of what had occurred between Vince and herself, she wanted to die with shame. Last night she could have accused him of rape, or something equally discrediting, but this time she could find no accusation to fling at him. He had been savage in his demands, but gentle in his conquering, and she had been so desperately eager to please him. *Why?* The question stabbed mercilessly at her mind. *Why* had she been so terribly eager to please a man who was merely using her as a weapon with which to hurt her father? There had to be an explanation somewhere, but Cara was inexplicably afraid to search for it. She brushed her hair instead, and pushed her feet into her ruined sandals before leaving the cottage.

Cara found Vince some distance beyond the place where she had fallen into the river that morning. He was standing inside a square of wrought-iron fencing, and his fair head was bowed as he leaned with one hand against a square concrete pillar which tapered into a point at the pinnacle. He was obviously lost in thought, and she was convinced that he was unaware of her presence. He turned his head sharply when she called his name, and for one flash of a second she glimpsed a look of such deep suffering in his eyes that she instinctively wanted to comfort him.

'Stay where you are!' he barked out a command when her hand went out towards the catch on the gate, and the unexpected ring of hatred in his voice was enough to freeze her on the spot.

'Is this your father's grave?' she asked intuitively, determined not to let him see how much it had hurt her to know that this was forbidden territory for the daughter of David Lloyd.

'Yes, it is,' he confirmed abruptly.

'Wasn't it rather risky of you to select this spot?' she questioned him, her glance shifting calculatively towards the river not six metres away. 'Have you never considered the possibility that the river might rise if there should be a flood?'

'It's unlikely that the river will rise higher than the base of this column, and there's nothing beneath this coil which could be damaged,' he explained coldly, pointing to the brass plate fastened to the column. 'My father's ashes are behind this plaque.'

Cara stared at it and read the brief inscription in silence. *In memory of our father—Siegfried Steiner*. This was followed by the date of his birth, and the date on which he had died almost eighteen years ago.

'Why did you bring his ashes here?' Cara asked curiously.

'My father loved this place, and the owner at that time gave us permission to come here. We used to do a lot of fishing here in the river when I was a boy.' Vince stepped out of the enclosure. He shut the gate firmly behind him, and gestured towards an ancient willow on the river's edge. 'We used to sit under that tree, and we used to talk and dream of the future. We still had a future then, and we still had our dreams, but your father took that privilege away from us.'

Cara felt a coldness shifting into her veins as she stared up at Vince and croaked, 'What are you saying?'

'He also took our pride and self-respect,' Vince turned on her with a savage fury burning in his eyes, 'and I shall never forgive David Lloyd for that.'

Her eyes widened in distress. 'For God's sake, Vince, what are you talking about?'

'I'm talking about your father!' he snarled. 'And I'm talking about how he changed us overnight from a respectable family to one that was condemned and ridiculed publicly.'

'There must be some mistake,' she cried desperately, and his mouth twisted in a cruel semblance of a smile.

'There is no mistake, believe me.'

Cara was stunned, and it seemed quite impossible to her that they could be talking about the same man. 'My father would never deliberately do anything to hurt anyone.'

'He succeeded very well in destroying my father, and he's going to pay very dearly for that,' Vince brushed aside her defence harshly, and he turned from her to stride back to the cottage as if he could not bear the sight of her.

Cara was momentarily too shattered to react, and several seconds passed before she followed him at a running pace. Indignation and anger gave her speed, and they arrived at the cottage simultaneously.

'Vince!' She leapt in front of him, gripping his arms urgently, and barring his way when he would have stepped inside. 'I want to know exactly what my father is being accused of.'

'I don't wish to discuss it with you,' he barked, brushing off her hands and attempting to pass her, but she barred his way once again, and raised blazing eyes to his.

'How can you make accusations, and then not want to verify them?'

A nerve jumped in his cheek, but other than that his face remained expressionless. 'I have all the proof I need, and I don't need to verify my accusations to you, or anyone else.'

'And is it your intention that I should also pay for whatever it is my father did?' the burning query burst unbidden from her lips.

His cold eyes raked her from head to foot, and there was not the slightest sign of softening when he said coldly, 'You are the daughter, are you not?'

Cara's face paled as if he had struck her, and his hands felt like branding irons on her shoulders when he set her aside and entered the cottage.

Blinded by a rush of stinging, incomprehensible tears, she leaned against the outer wall beside the door, and fought desperately against the pain of knowing that, to Vince, she would never be anything but the daughter of the man he despised. It had been a glaring truth all along, but after the intimacies they had shared she had thought ... what? That he might think a little differently of her? She straightened and dashed away

her tears. It was silly to stand there crying, and she had
to pull herself together. She had to think rationally, and
she had to try and make some sense out of this awful
thing which Vince had accused her father of.

The atmosphere in the cottage was strained and
tense. They made lunch together, and Vince surprised
her with his adeptness in the kitchen, but their
conversation was stilted. Cara wished that she could
hate Vince, but unfortunately that was not so easy. It
was not in her nature to carry the burden of hatred
around with her, and most especially not when she was
beginning to acknowledge the good points in the
character of the man she had initially disliked. Vince
was an enigma; an unknown quantity, and the more
time she spent with him, the more he intrigued her.

She sighed inwardly. It was a beautiful day, as Vince
had said, but they had both contributed something
towards spoiling it, and she felt curiously empty inside
when they drove back to Murrayville after lunch. She
glanced at his capable hands resting lightly on the
steering wheel, and she felt again their sensuous warmth
against her flesh. His expertise as a lover was
undeniable, but he obviously had a heart as cold as a
concrete slab. Was there perhaps too much hatred
inside him to leave any room for caring?

That night they once again had dinner alone. The
servants came and went in much the same silence that
reigned between Vince and Cara, and their efficiency
made Cara realise that Vince's home was run on a basis
which did not need a stay-at-home wife. To intrude on
the proceedings would merely disrupt the smoothness
with which everything was accomplished, and Cara
resolved not to interfere. She would, after all, be Vince's
wife for no more than a year, and that did not exactly
put her in a position where she had the right to make

changes in his home. The situation suited her perfectly. She could continue with her job at the library and her life would go on almost in the same way as before, but she could not ignore the fact that she was now bound to Vince Steiner. Being his wife, and all it entailed, no longer terrified her, but it did arouse a certain bitterness.

Vince excused himself after dinner and closeted himself in his study while Cara went upstairs. She needed an early night, but when she finally slid between the sheets she could not sleep. She tried to read, but the words danced meaningless before her eyes until she shut the book agitatedly.

Where was Vince? Was he going to remain in his study all night? *Did she care?* She slammed the book down on the bedside cupboard and snapped off the light.

A difficult day lay ahead of her; she would have to face the Murrayville public as *Mrs Steiner*, and she went hot and cold at the thought. John Curtis would have returned after a brief holiday at the coast, and he would be taking the position as manager to one of his father's new hotels. What was she going to tell *him*? Would he believe her if she told him that, during his two week absence, she had fallen madly in love with Vince Steiner? Cara did not think so. On several occasions, when they had attended the same function as Vince, she had made it abundantly clear that she could not tolerate the man who seemed to follow every movement she made with his piercing grey eyes. John would know that she was lying, and that was going to make things awkward.

The sound of footsteps in the passage made her stiffen in bed, but the door which was opened was the one across the passage. Incredulity shot through her, and it was followed by something quite indefinable. Vince was going to spend the night in the room across the passage. She ought to rejoice, but instead it felt as if she had been slapped in the face. Extraordinary! She must be going crazy ... or was it perhaps something much worse?

It was a long time before Cara went to sleep, and not before there was a dampness on her pillow for which she despised herself. Vince Steiner did not deserve her tears!

CHAPTER FIVE

'GOOD morning, Miss Lloyd,' Nancy de Witt greeted Cara in her customary manner, her head appearing round the door to Cara's office, but on this occasion she blushed profusely at her error and hastily corrected herself. 'I mean . . . Mrs Steiner.'

Mrs Steiner. It was the first time someone had called her that, and it sent an odd little shiver up her spine.

'Good morning, Nancy.' Cara forced a smile to her lips as she waved the young girl into the chair on the opposite side of her desk. 'Anything to report?'

'There have been several enquiries from children needing information for school projects.' Nancy passed Cara the sheet of paper on which she had made the necessary notes, and Cara glanced at the information jotted down in Nancy's neat handwriting. *Architecture of the Renaissance period; The Elizabethan Theatre; Van Gogh, the Artist and the Man.* 'We can also expect a large consignment of new books to arrive later this morning.' Nancy added with a cheerfulness which was galling on that particular Monday morning.

'Did those books have to arrive today of all days,' Cara groaned, leaning back in her chair and scowling up at the white-washed ceiling.

'I'm sorry, Mrs Steiner.'

'It's not your fault, Nancy, and don't pay any attention to me,' Cara brushed aside her apology, and she sat up again with a tight smile on her lips. 'I'm simply not in the mood for all that cataloguing.'

'And especially not when you ought to be on your honeymoon,' Nancy added innocently.

Her sympathy was misplaced, and Cara knew a strange desire to laugh hysterically, but somehow she managed to maintain a sober expression. 'Yes, well . . . let's get on with what we have to do.'

Nancy's red curls bobbed about her elfin face when she nodded enthusiastically, and her step was bouncy when she walked out of Cara's office. Cara wished suddenly that she could match Nancy's enthusiasm, but instead she felt drained and exhausted at the mere thought of what lay ahead of them. The classification of three hundred books was a mountainous task which would encompass several extra hours of work for the next week or more. The library and its facilities had expanded enormously over the past year, and they desperately needed at least *one* extra woman to help out during the hours when the library was open to the public, but thus far the authorities would not hear of it. Cara had argued; she had even threatened, but all to no avail. They could not afford the wages for extra help on their low budget. That was the only reply Cara received, and nothing short of an explosion would dislodge the authorities from that decision.

The consignment of books arrived at a most inconvenient time that morning. The library had barely opened its doors to the public when the truck from the Provincial Library squealed to a halt at the entrance, and for the next two hours everything was chaotic. There was no time to pause for tea and, when the library doors closed at twelve, the real work began in earnest. Cara sent Nancy off to lunch at one, but she herself remained in the library to continue with the task of stacking books in the shelves kept exclusively for new arrivals which needed attention.

Cara stood perched high on a ladder with a pile of books balanced on the step in front of her, and she was totally absorbed in what she was doing when a familiar, deep-throated voice remarked, 'You have lovely legs, Mrs Steiner.'

Her breath jerked in her throat as she turned her head sharply to find herself looking down into Vince's rugged face and, her balance awry, she felt the ladder swaying beneath her.

'Careful!' he warned, raising his hands to steady her as well as the ladder, and his steadying grip on her hip was enough to set her pulse racing madly.

The last time she had seen him was when they had parted company after dinner the previous evening, and his presence now had such a disturbing impact on her that her knees felt as if they wanted to buckle beneath her weight.

'What arc you doing here?' she demanded coolly, her glance sliding over his wide shoulders beneath the grey-striped jacket of his immaculate suit.

'Don't you have a lunch hour?' he counter-questioned mockingly, releasing her when she was steady on the ladder.

'This *is* my lunch hour,' she said coldly, aware suddenly that she was displaying far too much of her stockinged legs for his inspection, but she was too afraid to move while this weakness in her knees persisted.

'Why don't you come down off that ladder and have lunch with me?'

'I can't.'

'Can't come off that ladder, or can't have lunch with me?' he mocked her, his glance deliberately sliding upwards from her slim ankles to beneath the skirt of her blue woollen dress.

'I can't have lunch with you,' she answered stiffly and, motivated into action, she climbed down the ladder, but when her feet touched the carpeted floor she wondered if it would not have been wiser to remain up there on the ladder. Vince was menacingly tall, and he was standing so close to her that her nostrils quivered with the scent of his particular brand of masculine cologne. It stirred her senses and threatened to shatter what was left of her composure. 'I have stacks of books to catalogue and, if I don't do so now, it will mean working late in the evenings,' she explained, despising herself for that little tremor in her voice.

'Are you going to take a break for a cup of tea before two o'clock?'

'Yes, I might,' she conceded reluctantly, raising her questioning glance to his.

'Make two cups of tea, and I'll go and get us a snack to have with it,' he ordered brusquely, and was gone before she could protest.

He was a strange man, she decided when she climbed up the ladder to resume her task. She could not forget what had occurred the day before. He had desired her one minute, and the next he had shown quite clearly that he despised her. Last night he had avoided her as if he could not stand the sight of her, and yet today he was going out of his way to share his lunch hour with her. A complex man, that's what Vince was, and she wondered if anyone would ever truly understand him.

Cara thrust him forcibly from her mind and concentrated on the pile of books in front of her. She sorted them carefully and stacked them in the shelf, but some minutes later she had a curious sensation that someone was watching her.

'John!' she exclaimed in delight and surprise when she turned her head and found herself looking down into John Curtis' lean face. His dark brown hair lay in its usual unruly fashion across his forehead, but his green eyes lacked that sparkling warmth she was accustomed to.

'Was that Vince Steiner I saw leaving the building a few minutes ago?' he questioned her in his smooth, pleasant voice when she had climbed down the ladder to plant a friendly, welcoming kiss on his cheek, and she realised at once the reason for his disturbed, almost stern expression.

'Yes, it was,' she answered quietly, and she was tense suddenly in the company of this man with whom she had never had reason to be anything but herself.

'It's true, then?' He thrust his hands into his pockets, hunching his lanky body, and peering intently down into her eyes. 'You're married to him?'

News had a way of travelling fast in Murrayville, she realised cynically, and she steeled herself for what was to follow. 'Yes, it's true.'

John's wide mouth was drawn into a thin, angry line. 'Don't tell me he swept you off your feet in a whirlwind romance, Cara, because I refuse to believe that.'

She winced inwardly at the bitterness in his voice. Had Vince been correct in his assumption that John felt more for her than simply friendship? Cara shut her mind hastily to this disquieting thought. John, I. . . .'

'Have you been forced into this marriage?' he demanded when words failed her, and it required a strenuous effort from her to adopt an outraged expression.

'No, of course not!'

'Look at me, Cara.' Slender-fingered hands gripped her shoulders and forced her to face him when she would have turned away, and the determined set of his jaw filled her with alarm. 'I happen to know there has been some deal on the go between Steiner and your father these past eighteen months. Does Steiner have some sort of hold on your father? Did he use it to blackmail you into marrying him?'

He had hit on the truth so accurately that she was momentarily speechless. How did John know of her father's dealings with Vince, when she, who had lived in the same house with her father, had had no idea of what was going on?

'My decision to marry Vince was a personal one.' There was some truth in that, she consoled herself, but to elaborate would prove her statement a lie.

'You're not in love with him. Don't expect me to believe that, Cara.'

It hurt to see the pain in his eyes, and she lowered her gaze to the knot in his striped tie. 'John, dear, I can't talk to you now, and I'm really very busy.'

His hands fell away from her, and his shoulders seemed to sag beneath the cut of his jacket. They had always been completely truthful with each other; that was what had strengthened their friendship, and having to lie to him made Cara feel like a traitor.

'You don't want to answer my questions for some reason,' he accused darkly. 'You're trying to fob me off with subterfuge.'

'She's trying to tell you to mind your own business,' Vince's harsh voice sliced into the awkward silence unexpectedly, and both John and Cara spun round to face him.

Anxiety and tension clutched with vice-like fingers at Cara's chest and throat when she studied the two men who stood facing each other like snarling opponents in an arena. John was tall and strong, but Vince was a head taller, and physically John's superior. They were unevenly matched, but John was not easily intimidated.

'You forced Cara into this marriage, Steiner, and I know it,' he accused without preamble, and Cara felt her stomach lurch with sickening fear when she saw the expression on Vince's face.

The muscles jutted out for an instant like boulders along the side of his jaw, but just as suddenly his features relaxed, and his steel-grey eyes actually glittered with mockery and humour when they met Cara's.

'When I proposed marriage, *liebchen*, was I holding a knife to your throat?' Vince questioned her smoothly.

How suave, how confident, and how despicably arrogant he was in his assumption that she would not let him down. He knew, *damn him*, that if she let him down she would also be humiliating herself. *Was I holding a knife to your throat?* he had asked. He had spoken figuratively, and the only way she could answer him truthfully was to do so literally.

'No,' she said, her voice admirably convincing. 'There was no knife held to my throat.'

'There you have your answer, Curtis,' Vince smiled coldly, turning back to John, and gesturing expressively as if the matter was settled.

John's scowling, questioning glance met Cara's, and she pleaded with him silently, her eyes begging him to accept the situation and to leave before something happened she would regret for the rest of her life. He looked a little stunned, almost as if he had understood, then he turned on his heel and walked out of the library without a backward glance.

Cara's eyes followed him out of the building, and a deep sadness settled like a sombre cloak about her. 'I hate what I've just done to John,' she murmured unhappily. 'He has been a good and loyal friend for many years, and I have repaid his loyalty and his friendship with subterfuge and lies.'

'I warn you, Cara,' Vince spoke threateningly beside her. 'Tell Curtis the truth about our marriage, and I cancel my agreement with your father at once,' He thrust a carton of sandwiches into her hands. 'Enjoy your lunch.'

Vince had almost reached the door before she found her voice. 'What about you?'

He did no hear her, or perhaps he had not wanted to hear her. He walked out and slammed the door behind him with a force that reverberated throughout the silent library.

Cara stared at her desk calendar. She had been married to Vince for almost three weeks, and during this time she had discovered more about the Steiner empire than about the man who had founded it. His temporary offices in Murrayville contained a bevy of staff that leapt to his command, and two or more days each week were spent at his headquarters in Johannesburg, or elsewhere. Cara never questioned him, and neither did he take her into his confidence where the nature of his work was concerned.

Their level of communication had, in fact, dropped almost to zero since that day he had walked into the library to find her with John Curtis, and their lives had settled into a pattern which was becoming more depressing with each passing day. There was never again a repetition of that night he had slept in the room across the passage from her own. When he was home they occupied the same bed, and Cara was driven to take the necessary precautions. If there was one thing she did not want, then it was to discover herself pregnant with his child. She suffered enough because of their loveless nights of passion, and to have his child would merely increase her suffering to an unbearable level.

Tears stung her eyes, and she blinked them away hastily. She could not understand herself. All she wanted to do lately was cry, and it was most confusing. She had always lived such an orderly and serene life, but there was nothing orderly about her chaotic existence these days, and the mere thought of Vince was enough to shatter her serenity. It was incredible. He had only to walk into a room and her nerves would react like the strings of a harp that had been plucked. She had tried to ignore him, but nearly always she had found herself observing him more closely, and instead of dreading those nights when he would come to her, she found that she was actually listening for his footsteps. Was she going crazy?

Cara had seen her parents quite often during the past three weeks, but there had never been the opportunity to speak to her father privately. Her mother was always there, making it impossible to speak confidentially, and Cara decided eventually that the only way to see him alone would be to ask him to come to her office at the library.

It had become imperative that she should confront him with the knowledge she had acquired from Vince, and she reached for the telephone on her desk. She dialled the familiar number, and David Lloyd answered almost at once, an unusual gruffness in his voice which tension and tiredness had put there.

'Please call in at the library some time today,' she said without wasting time on the usual pleasantries, and for several seconds there was a strained silence on the line.

'Is it urgent?' he asked eventually, and she detected a wariness in his voice which she was not accustomed to.

'I need to talk to you, Dad.'

Again there was that strained silence, but a faint sigh finally reached her ears. 'I'll see what I can do.'

Cara put down the receiver and leaned back in her chair. It had been easier than she had imagined, but the difficult part still lay ahead of her. There was so much she wanted to know, and she did not think that her father would part with his knowledge willingly.

David Lloyd did not come to the library until that afternoon. Cara was helping Nancy attend to the people at the counter when she saw her father walk in, and her heart gave a nervous little leap when she saw that now familiar tightness about his mouth.

'I'll be back in a few minutes, Nancy,' she apologised to the girl beside her and, lifting the counter, flap, she let herself out of the enclosure to walk towards her father. 'Come this way, Dad,' she said, taking his arm and leading him towards her office.

'Are you well, Cara?' he asked anxiously when he sat facing her in her small office. 'Steiner hasn't been ill-treating you, has he?'

Ill-treated! The words clattered through her mind, and stirred a feeling of hysteria. Her emotions had run the full scale from shocked fury to numbed acceptance during the past three weeks, but she could not accuse Vince of ill-treatment. She felt deeply hurt more than anything else, but the reason for it remained elusive, and this was not exactly the moment for a self-analysis.

'His name is Vince and, considering that he is my husband, it wouldn't sound nice if people should hear you speak of him as *Steiner*,' she reprimanded her father gently.

'It isn't easy thinking of him as my son-in-law.'

'How do you think of him, then?' she almost laughed when she met his sombre, grey-green glance.

'How I think of him is irrelevant,' he brushed aside the matter with a wave of his hand. 'What did you want to discuss with me?'

Cara took a moment to sort out the queries in her mind. She would have to handle the situation with extreme tact and care, and her mouth went dry with nervous anxiety.

'You borrowed money from Vince,' she began tentatively. 'Is that all there is between you, or is there something else which I don't know about?'

She saw her father start. 'What do you mean?'

'Is there something you haven't told me, Dad?'

'Are you suggesting that I am hiding things from you?'

His voice was indignant, but his hands were shaking, and a sheen of perspiration stood out on his forehead despite the coolness in her office. *Tell me*, she pleaded silently. *Tell me what you did to Siegfried Steiner and his family that has made Vince indulge in this terrible desire for revenge?*

'I'm not suggesting anything, Dad,' she said instead in a deliberately calm voice. 'I'm merely asking if there is something else between you and Vince other than the loan; something that happened in the past, perhaps.'

David Lloyd stood up abruptly and turned towards the door. 'I don't think I want to continue this discussion.'

'I'd hate this to sound like emotional blackmail,' she stopped him before he could leave, 'but I think I have earned the right to know everything there is to know about your association with Vince.'

'What makes you think that there is something you don't know?' he asked, turning slowly to face her, and his cheeks had gone strangely ashen.

'You're playing verbal hide and seek with me, Dad,'

she accused with a hint of impatience in her husky voice. 'Vince is burning up inside with the desire for revenge, and you cringe every time his name is mentioned. There is more to this than simply the loan which you couldn't pay back at the stipulated time, and I think it's only fair that I know about it.'

David Lloyd reached for the chair with a hand that shook and sat down heavily. He looked mentally and physically defeated, and Cara felt her concern for him spiralling. He wiped the perspiration off his forehead with his handkerchief and lit a cigarette, but he puffed at it furiously as if he was afraid he would not get enough smoke into his lungs.

'I made a grave error of judgment once, and it is not something I'm very proud of,' he confessed grimly. 'More than that I'm not prepared to say at the moment.'

Tell me! her mind screamed at him. *Tell me it's not true that you ruined Vince's father!*

'Did you know Siegfried Steiner?' she asked at length, her jaw tight, and her insides considerably tighter.

'Yes, I knew him.'

Did she imagine it, or had her father gone a shade paler with that admission? 'If you knew Vince's father, then you must also know that he is no longer alive.'

'Siegfried Steiner died almost eighteen years ago.' He puffed agitatedly on his cigarette and finally crushed the remainder into the ashtray on her desk. 'Look, Cara, I can't discuss this at the moment. It's all very complicated and involved and painful, and ... and every man has to pay for his sins one way or the other.'

Incredulity washed over her like a thousand pin pricks. 'Vince wants revenge, and you're letting him have it?'

'I suppose you could say so, yes.'

Cara felt a surge of uncontrollable anger rising within her. 'So I have been sacrificed on the altar of your guilt.'

'Don't say that!'

'But it's the truth!' she argued as he leapt to his feet in protest. 'Oh, I know I more or less sealed my own fate by walking into your study that evening, and I know I have only myself to blame, but you let it all happen without actually lifting a finger to prevent it.'

David Lloyd sat down heavily once again and lit another cigarette with nicotine-stained fingers that shook. 'I had no choice. Your mother——'

'Yes, I know,' she interrupted coldly. She was seeing her father for the first time as he really was, and she could barely conceal her disappointment. She had thought him strong, but he was weak; she had imagined that she could rely on him, but when it came to saving his own skin he had not objected overmuch at making use of his own daughter. 'You have always wanted to protect Mother from the unpleasant things in life, but I'm beginning to think that you have been totally unfair in your judgment of her character,' Cara accused, suddenly immensely tired, but restless to a degree that drove her to her feet to stand at the window watching the municipal workers raking up the leaves which had fallen on to the lawns and pavements. She was raking just as they were, but she was raking into her father's personality as well as the past, and it was not particularly pleasant. 'I often wonder how Mother would have reacted if you had confronted her with all the problems you have so carefully hidden from her. Would she have cracked under the strain, or would she have proved that she is a woman of strength and character?' Cara spoke without turning.

The chair behind her creaked, and the next moment

her father's heavy hand rested on her shoulder. 'Cara. . . .'

'Do you know something, Dad?' she forestalled him. 'I think it was wrong of you not to give her the opportunity to demonstrate exactly what she's made of, and I think if you had you would have been pleasantly surprised.'

'Lilian is a fiercely loyal and a very just woman.' He turned Cara to face him, and she was shocked at the bleak despair she saw in his eyes. 'You take after your mother, Cara, and I'm not proud of myself for what I have done to you. I would have protected you from this marriage if it had been at all possible, but I confess to thinking selfishly only of myself and, short of committing murder, there was really nothing I could do. I needed time and, God knows, I need this new contract more than I've ever needed anything before in my life.'

This last statement lingered in Cara's mind long after her father had gone. He had needed the time her marriage to Vince would give him, and he needed this new contract for the new steel plant even more desperately. What if he did not get it? She went cold at the thought, but it was a possibility she had to face.

A red Porsche stood parked in the driveway when Cara arrived at the house late that afternoon, and she glanced at it curiously when she had parked her grey Mini in the garage alongside Vince's Mercedes. Did they have guests for the weekend, or was Vince entertaining a business associate? The latter did not seem quite possible. Vince had once informed her that he never dealt with business matters outside his office. This was, however, a rule he had bent a little where it concerned his dealings with her father.

Jackson opened the door for Cara and wished her a

pleasant 'good-evening' when she stepped into the hall. Short, stocky, and black as coal dust, Cara had nicknamed him *Jack-of-all-trades*. He acted as butler, chauffeur, and steward at their stable, and on occasion she had actually seen him pottering around in the garden.

'The master is in the living-room, Madam,' he announced when he had relieved her of her coat, and she hastily checked her appearance in the mirror of the antique hallstand.

Laughter, clear as a bell and very feminine, drew Cara towards the door which stood slightly ajar, and she pushed it open farther to enter the spacious room where a welcoming fire burned in the grate of the fireplace. In the chair facing Vince sat a woman who could have stepped out of the pages of a *Vogue* magazine. She wore a wide-sleeved, grey striped dress and, to relieve the severity of the colour, she had tied a crimson scarf about her throat. Her chestnut-coloured hair had a touch of fire in it that matched the fire in her green eyes, and the crimson mouth was curved in a smile that suggested she was fully aware of the elegant and sophisticated image she projected.

'Ah, *liebchen*, I would like you to meet Chantal Webber,' Vince did the necessary introductions in his deep-throated, suave manner. 'Chantal, this is my wife, Cara.'

Vince had risen to his feet, but Chantal Webber had remained seated, her slender, carefully manicured hand extended politely towards Cara. 'How nice to meet you, my dear.' Her voice was warm as honey taken that moment from the hive, but her limp hand was cool when Cara clasped it briefly. 'I can't tell you how surprised I was when I heard that Vince was married, but now I can see why he wasted no time in securing you to his side.'

Chantal Webber could afford to be charitable, Cara thought dismally. Never before had she seen one woman endowed with so much beauty, and she was suddenly conscious of the fact that her own appearance left much to be desired. The breeze outside had whipped a strand of hair out of place, and there had not been time during the course of the afternoon to touch up her make-up. Her neat, pale blue suit had stamp pad ink smudged on the sleeve of the jacket, and her hands felt grubby after handling dusty filing cards and books.

'Chantal will be staying the weekend,' Vince informed Cara with a smile on his lips which did not match the glacier coldness in his eyes.

'I'll tell the servants to prepare the guest room,' Cara replied stiffly, seeking a reason to escape.

'I have already instructed the servants to do so,' Chantal intervened. 'I have always done so in the past, and I didn't think you would object if I did so now.'

Oh, didn't you? Cara thought cynically, an icy anger slicing through her. Who the hell was in charge of this household; Vince's mistress, or his wife? *Silly question.* Cara was his wife for a year, but Chantal had been his mistress, and she would continue to be his mistress once their marriage was dissolved.

'I am pleased to see you are making yourself at home as I'm sure you have always done.' Cara's voice was cool but polite to the extreme. 'Excuse me, but I would like to go up and change.'

'I shall have a sherry waiting for you, *liebchen*, so don't be too long,' Vince warned.

She caught a look in his eyes when she passed his chair. Was it mockery, or anger? Whatever it was, it warned her that she would have to take more care not to make her feelings so obvious.

Cara bathed and changed into her favourite dress. It

was a floral mixture of amber and golden brown, and it accentuated the creamy smoothness of her skin. The material was warm and gossamer soft to the touch, while the softly cowled neckline added an elegant finish to an otherwise plain style. She had brushed her hair and had coiled it into its usual knot, but for tonight she chose an ivory comb to hold it in place. Tiny diamond studs sparkled in her ears, and she payed a little more attention than usual to her make-up when she thought of the beautiful Chantal Webber in the living-room with Vince.

She felt slightly more confident when she joined them some minutes later, but she sipped her sherry in silence while they discussed incidents involving people Cara had no knowledge of. She felt like an unwelcome third intruding on a private conversation, but she was not going to scuttle off like a wounded rabbit to some corner of the house. Vince glanced at her during a lull in the conversation, and his eyes glittered strangely when they flicked over her. It was infuriating that she could never quite tell what he was thinking. Was he comparing her to that ravishing beauty who had held his attention for the past half hour? Cara glanced at Chantal, and something in those sparkling green eyes told her that this woman was not terribly thrilled with the idea that Vince had married someone else. Those heavily lashed eyes narrowed perceptibly to assess the enemy in preparation to do battle, and Cara almost laughed out loud. *If only Chantal knew.*

Jackson came in to announce that dinner was to be served, and Cara breathed an inward sigh of relief. She knew that she looked calm and confident, but there was something about Chantal Webber which was decidedly unsettling at that precise moment.

CHAPTER SIX

CHANTAL sparkled at the dinner table. She succeeded in drawing Vince out from behind that barrier he had built around himself, and Cara was quite content to sit and watch his harsh features soften occasionally into a smile which she felt certain would never be directed at her. A searing stab of pain shot through her, but she chose to ignore it. There would be enough time later to wonder about it.

'Vince tells me you are a librarian,' Chantal directed her remark at Cara when they were having their dessert, and Cara was suddenly uncomfortable at having both Chantal and Vince's attention focused on herself.

'That's correct,' Cara managed stiffly.

'You find it interesting working among a lot of dusty old books?' Chantal questioned scornfully, and Cara felt her back stiffen defensively.

'Our books are neither old, nor dusty, and I have always thrived on literature of any kind.'

'You studied literature?'

Cara had no wish to discuss her achievements, but she could not avoid answering Chantal's pertinent questions. 'I have a university degree, yes.'

'How very clever you must be, Cara, but men do not always pay much attention to a woman's brain.' Chantal smiled with a galling sweetness as she tilted her head at Vince. 'It is the female anatomy men find so much more attractive, is that not so, Vince, darling?'

Steel-hard mockery glittered in his eyes when he directed his gaze at Cara's rigid features. 'The female body is there for the delight of men, and if the lady in question happens to be clever, then I imagine some men would consider that a bonus.'

The conversation was veering towards the personal, and Cara felt as if she was floundering in unfamiliar water, but her voice was cool and faintly sarcastic when she spoke. 'I can't imagine that you would consider that a bonus, Vince.'

'Quite frankly, I haven't given it much thought.' His eyes burned their way sensuously down towards the soft outline of her breasts, and they lingered there deliberately. 'Tomorrow we will have been married three weeks, and to this day it is still your body that interests me.'

Cara felt the sting of humiliation in her cheeks, and Chantal's tinkling laughter merely added insult to injury.

'Do not let him fool you, Cara, into believing he will ever find pleasure in the grey matter between your ears,' she explained unnecessarily. 'Vince is very much a man's man, and he considers that women serve only one purpose.'

Vince's eyebrows rose in sardonic amusement. 'Are you trying to frighten my wife into believing that I am a sex fiend, Chantal?'

'I am not trying to frighten her at all,' Chantal laughed coquettishly, placing her slender hand on his arm in a gesture of familiarity which Cara was beginning to dislike intensely. 'I was merely telling the truth, and you know it,' Chantal added with another little laugh.

Vince and Chantal smiled at each other as if they were sharing a personal joke, and that odd stab of pain shot through Cara once again.

'Could I offer you more dessert?' Cara broke the

brief silence, and she placed the bowl of soufflé within Chantal's reach.

'How very tactfully your wife changes the subject,' Chantal smiled into Vince's eyes before she turned to Cara. 'No, thank you, I don't think I shall have more dessert, Cara. I must watch my figure, or a certain man I know will not be wanting to look at me again in future.'

Her green glance darted swiftly and meaningfully towards Vince, and Cara felt a little sick inside. 'Shall we have coffee in the living-room?'

'A good idea,' Vince agreed, placing his table napkin beside his plate and pushing back his chair.

The living-room had been warmed beautifully by the fire, and Jackson served their coffee the moment they had made themselves comfortable in the chairs arranged close to the fireplace.

Vince swallowed down a mouthful of black coffee and glanced from Chantal to Cara. 'Shall we go out to the cottage tomorrow and spend the day there?'

'What a wonderful idea, Vince,' Chantal replied before Cara could do so. 'I was hoping you would suggest it.'

Vince directed his questioning gaze at Cara. 'How do you feel about it, *liebchen?*'

'I'm afraid I'm on duty at the library tomorrow,' she answered stiffly, 'but please don't let that stop you from going out to the cottage.'

She was playing right into Chantal's hands, but she told herself that she did not care. Her excuse was legitimate, and it was up to Vince to decide what they would do.

'Is it imperative that you work tomorrow?' he demanded of Cara.

'I am on duty every alternate Saturday, if you remember.'

Vince's jaw hardened. 'I am sure that if you explained to Nancy she would be only too willing to accommodate you and work tomorrow.'

Bright green eyes observed them in calculated silence, and Cara could not help thinking that Chantal was waiting like a vulture to get into the final act.

'There is nothing to stop me from asking Nancy to stand in for me, but that would be unfair,' Cara explained, her chin set with determination. 'Nancy has made her own arrangements for this weekend, and I have no intention of asking her to alter them at this stage.'

'You are being deliberately obstinate,' Vince accused with a harshness that made Cara wince inwardly, and at this point the vulture swooped down from her perch.

'Vince, darling, you are behaving like a dictator,' Chantal accused in a voice as sweet as treacle. 'If Cara has to work tomorrow, then there is nothing you can do about it and, if she does not mind, then why shouldn't you and I go out there to the cottage for the day.' That sparkling green gaze was once again directed at Cara. 'You really don't mind, do you, my dear?'

Cara felt her insides curl into a tight ball of displeasure. There was no sense of deluding herself; she *hated* the idea of Vince and Chantal spending the entire day alone at the cottage, but she hid her feelings behind a cool, tranquil mask.

'I don't mind at all,' she lied smoothly.

'There you are, then,' Chantal smiled triumphantly at Vince. 'Everything is settled without all the unnecessary fuss.'

Cara felt Vince's glacier glance resting on her, but she refused to look at him, and kept her eyes lowered to the cup of coffee in her hands. Chantal discussed her plans for the following day with enthusiasm, but Cara was no longer listening. She felt cold and miserable despite the warmth of the fire, and, when the clock on the mantelshelf struck nine, she swallowed down the last mouthful of coffee and rose to her feet.

'If you would excuse me, I've had an incredibly busy day, and I'd like to go to bed.'

'Of course we shall excuse you,' Chantal said at once, and her smile told Cara that this woman was anxious to be alone with Vince.

'I'll be up a little later,' Vince announced, his face an unfathomable mask, and Cara bid them both 'good-night'.

Cara's head was pounding and her legs felt as if they had been stuffed with lead when she went up the stairs. She *was* tired, but that weightiness in her body was something new to her. In the bedroom she worked her way through her nightly ritual like an automaton, taking off her clothes and slipping into a silky nightgown. She took the diamond studs out of her earlobes and placed them neatly in their velvet-lined box before she creamed the make-up off her face. Her eyes in the mirror looked shadowed and suddenly much too large in her pale face. She looked twice her age and felt it too, she told herself, and her eyes smarted with those tears which came so easily lately. Cara dashed them away angrily with the back of her hand, and pulled the ivory comb from her hair to let it cascade down her back like a glossy black curtain. It had never been a chore to brush her hair each night before going to bed, but this was one night when she wished that her hair was shorter and easier to manage. Her arms felt heavy with a strange fatigue, and the brush had slipped twice from her fingers before she had finished brushing her hair.

Vince was downstairs in the living-room with

Chantal. What were they doing? The images that flashed through her mind brought back that stab of pain, and still she refused to analyse it. 'Later . . . some other time . . . not now!' she told herself. She was too tired, and too tense to think straight.

One seemingly endless hour passed before Vince entered the bedroom. Cara heard him swearing in the darkness when he knocked his shin against a chair, but she hoped that he would think she was asleep. She supposed that she ought to feel flattered that he had come to *her* bedroom instead of Chantal's, but all she felt at that moment was resentment.

The bed sagged beneath his weight, and she felt a rush of cool air against her body before his arms reached for her. There was no longer any sense in pretending that she was asleep. Vince somehow always knew when she was feigning, and her body grew taut against the whipcord strength of his muscular frame.

'No!' she protested when his lips sought hers.

'Yes!' he laughed throatily, his hand sliding down to the hollow of her back and drawing her closer to the grinding hardness of his hips.

Her treacherous body responded with a leap of hot, clamouring emotions, but her mind was filled with cold rejection. 'Do you have to pester me every night?'

'You are my wife, or have you forgotten?'

'I wish to hell I wasn't your wife!' she snapped.

'Come now, *liebchen*,' his deep voice mocked her. 'You know you enjoy our little bedtime romp together.'

Cara blessed the darkness when a fiery heat swept into her face. 'You're the most conceitedly arrogant man I have ever had the misfortune to meet. You disgust me, and I wish you would leave me alone.'

'Would you rather I spend the night with our lovely guest?' he mocked her, his warm mouth against her throat kindling exquisite fires, and his hand sliding upwards beneath the silky garment to caress her smooth, shapely thigh.

Oh God! Why did she have to feel so weak ... so wanton! Her body was clearly begging him to fill that aching void inside her, but her mind coldly dictated the words that spilled from her lips.

'I couldn't care less whether you spent the night with Chantal, or elsewhere, just as long as it isn't here with me,' she croaked, and his hand ceased its arousing caress to bite cruelly into her hip.

'I will give you five seconds to deny that statement,' he warned, raising his head so that she could see the glittering hardness in his eyes in the moonlight filtering in through the window. 'One ... two ...'

'You may count yourself into hell for all I care!' she cried out determinedly, but something inside her was shouting a dire warning which she was tooo agitated to heed.

'Three ... four ...'

'You're wasting your breath.'

'Five. . . .' The ominous silence following that last count was filled suddenly with the hard, anxious beat of her heart before he released her and got out of the bed to put on his robe. 'You will regret this, Cara, and don't say I didn't warn you.'

His words hovered in the air like a sinister threat as he strode out of the room and closed the door behind him. She felt as if she had turned to stone for a moment, then she leapt out of bed, and she was shivering inexplicably when she reached the door. Every instinct within her dictated that she should call him back to her side, and she opened the door with a fumbling hand, but the words that surged into her throat remained locked there at the sound of Vince knocking loudly on the guest-room door.

Cara froze. She could not believe this was actually happening, and she was still standing there in an incredulous stupor when Chantal's voice reached her ears. 'Vince, darling, I did not expect you to come to me when your lovely wife——'

Chantal's exclamation of surprise was stifled, and Cara could imagine in what way. The sound of the guest-room door being closed ripped through Cara like a knife tearing into her flesh, and she closed her own door hastily. A wailing siren had been set off in her mind and she pressed her palms against her throbbing temples. *Oh, God, what have I done!*

Her breath was coming in choking sobs, but her eyes were dry as that searing, stabbing pain pierced her to her very soul. She could not ignore it now; it was sheer unadulterated jealousy, and everything inside her seemed to split wide open. The naked truth was thrust upon her with a force that left her numb and shaken. She was in love with Vince, and she knew now that she had loved him almost from the first moment she had seen him. Instinct had warned that he was a threat to her peaceful existence, and antagonism had been the barrier behind which she had sought protection. To help her father out of his financial difficulties, and to save the home her mother loved, she had been forced to marry Vince, but the callousness of his demands had strengthened the protective armour she had erected about her heart.

Cara recognised at last the feelings she had hidden so well that even she had not suspected, but the truth had taken too long in revealing itself. It was too late! *Much* too late!

She stumbled across the room and fell on to the bed to bury her face in the pillow with an anguished cry on her lips. Only then did the tears come; hot, stinging tears that brought no relief to her soul while her mind conjured up cruel visions of Vince and Chantal locked in a passionate embrace.

The house was silent when Cara went down to breakfast the following morning. Instead of her usual bacon and eggs she settled for toast and coffee, and if Jackson thought it strange, then he did not comment on it. The skilful appliance of make-up hid the outward signs of her long, turbulent night, but inwardly she felt crushed and bruised. Last night Vince had warned that she would regret her actions, but she had never dreamed that he would actually go from her bed to Chantal's. Only Vince could have devised such a cruel punishment, and she knew that the pain of it was something she would have to bear for the rest of her life.

She bit into a slice of toast. It was warm and crisp, but when she tried to swallow it, it felt like a piece of lead lodged in her throat. She washed it down with a mouthful of coffee, and she left the rest of her toast untouched.

'Good morning, Cara.' Vince had come in so silently that she had not heard him, and she found herself staring at him as if she had never seen him before. His black slacks and sweater were a perfect foil for his sun-bleached hair and tanned features, and those icy-grey eyes seemed to take in every detail of her appearance even as she was taking in his. He pulled out a chair, and the expensive material of his slacks strained across his thigh muscles when he sat down close to her. She wanted to hate him for looking so calm and for behaving as if nothing had happened, but instead she found herself loving him with every fibre of her being. He placed an empty cup in front of him, and gestured towards the coffee pot. 'Is that coffee still warm?'

The scent of his aftershave lotion tantalised her

senses, but she pulled herself together sharply. 'It's warm enough.'

He poured himself a cup of coffee and drank it without adding milk or sugar. Did he spend the entire night with Chantal, or did he leave her after he had had his fill of her? Oh, God, why did she have to torture herself with these agonising thoughts? Vince could not care less about her. She was standing in as security for her father's loan, and even in marriage she was the pawn Harriet had spoken of; the pawn in his ruthless game of revenge.

'I trust you slept well, *liebchen*?'

Liebchen! How dare he call her *liebchen* after what he had done to her last night! She felt degraded, insulted, and humiliated, and she would never forgive him for it. *Never!*

'I slept very well, thank you,' she replied tritely, avoiding his probing glance for fear that those razor sharp eyes might glimpse her pain and distress.

'I had a very good night as well, in case you wanted to know,' he informed her smoothly, and she had an uncommonly savage desire to claw out his eyes in an attempt to ease the pain and jealousy that seared through her.

'I'm not exactly interested.'

'Aren't you?'

The mockery in his voice sliced through her lie and pierced her soul. She had only herself to blame, but, oh God, what a price to pay for her folly.

'I have to go,' she said through stiff lips, pushing back her chair and getting to her feet before she made a complete fool of herself by bursting into tears.

'Before you go there is something you ought to know.' Fear, unreasonable and acute, was like an icy hand clutching at her heart, but somehow she turned to face him and steeled herself for whatever was to follow. 'Don't expect us home until late tonight. Chantal always plans a surprise meal for the evenings when we go out to the cottage, and in the past we seldom ate early.'

Relief and pain mingled and coiled itself into an unbearable knot at the pit of her stomach. She had no idea what she had expected, but she had a nagging suspicion she had feared she was going to be thrust out of his life. Perhaps that was what he had wanted her to think, and anger gave her the strength to face him coldly and calmly.

'Thanks for telling me, but don't expect me to wait up for you.'

His derisive smile was like the thrust of a knife in her heart. 'I never imagined you were the kind of wife who would be concerned enough to wait up for her husband.'

'In that case we understand each other perfectly,' she snapped icily, picking up her handbag. 'Enjoy your day.'

'I always enjoy the time I spend with Chantal, thank you,' his voice followed her as she left the room, and that knife in her heart was twisted with a savagery that would have made her cry out in agony had she not clenched her teeth until her jaw began to ache.

She crossed the hall, walking blindly, but a musical voice made her spin round as if she was no longer in control of her own body.

'Good morning,' Chantal smiled as she descended the stairs, and Cara felt a coldness invade her body which deadened all feeling.

The shaft of sunlight from the window above the door put fire into that shoulder-length chestnut hair, and her emerald green trouser suit enhanced the colour of her green eyes. Chantal Webber was beautiful. Her slender, perfectly proportioned body moved as if it spoke a sensuous language of its own, and Cara had no difficulty in discovering why Vince was so attracted to this woman. Together they were a striking couple, but at that moment Cara could not even conjure up a feeling of envy.

'Don't you regret your decision not to join us today?' Chantal asked, her high-heeled, calf-skin boots making no sound on the carpeted floor in the hall, and her calculating glance studying Cara intently.

'I have to work this morning, and that's all there is to it,' Cara replied, her voice abrupt and cool. 'Have a nice day.'

'Oh, we will,' Chantal laughed softly, and Cara wondered when she walked out of the house whether she had been mistaken in thinking she had heard a note of triumph in Chantal's laughter.

Cara got into her Mini and drove away from the house, but in her mind she could see Vince and Chantal having breakfast together. Were they talking together softly and intimately, and laughing about his frigid wife who had so uncaringly thrust them into each other's arms the night before?

A hot wave of pain and humiliation swept through her, and her hands tightened on the steering wheel until her knuckles shone white through the skin.

Damn Vince for stooping so low in his quest for revenge, and *damn* them both for what they did to her last night, she cursed them in silent fury, and then she cursed herself. The most idiotic thing she had ever done in her life was to fall in love with Vince. He was not worthy of such feelings, and she would not waste her time nurturing her love for him while knowing that he could never love her in return.

Cara could not concentrate on her work that

morning. She stamped cards, assisted new members to join, and answered queries, but only a part of her mind was on what she was doing. She thought about Vince and Chantal at the cottage out on the farm, and she could imagine them strolling along the side of the river on this warm Saturday morning. Would they make love eventually on that comfortable bed she had seen in the bedroom, or would they prefer the carpet in front of the fire?

'That's right, Cara,' she told herself fiercely while she was shoving books into the shelves. 'Go ahead and torture yourself until you're wallowing in self-pity.'

She had to stop thinking and feeling. At breakfast that morning she had thought that every scrap of feeling inside her was dead, but she had been wrong. She was hurting again, and the pain was more intense than before.

It was a long morning, the longest she had ever encountered, and when at last she arrived at the house she found that she could not face the lunch Jackson had prepared for her. She could, of course, change her mind and drive out to the farm to spend the afternoon and the evening with Vince and Chantal, but common sense warned that her Mini was too old to risk such a journey. She changed into warm slacks and a sweater and sat down miserably on the bed. The silence in the house had never disturbed her before, but now it was driving her slowly mad, and she decided on an impulse to spend the afternoon and evening with her parents. It might not even be a bad idea to sleep there. Vince and Chantal would return late that night, but Cara could not bear the thought of spending another night in that house such as the one she had spent the night before.

She flung her toiletries, nightgown, a change of clothing into a small bag, and she scribbled a brief note to

Vince which she left on the small cupboard beside the bed. Ten minutes later she was driving through town once again and heading towards her parent's home.

David and Lilian never questioned Cara as to her decision to spend the night with them. They simply took it for granted that Vince was away for the weekend, and Cara left it at that. It eased the hurt a little to be with her parents, but pain and depression took its toll that evening when they sat around the fire in the living-room. She found herself wondering what Vince and Chantal were doing, and the tears were suddenly much too close for comfort. She dared not cry in front of her parents. They would ask questions which she could not answer, and she was much too exhausted to put up a false front. Cara stared into the dancing flames of the fire and forced herself to think of something pleasant, but all she could see was Vince's sun-bronzed face.

She almost sighed audibly with relief when her mother announced at ten o'clock that she was going to bed. It gave Cara an excuse to do the same, but she was a little concerned about her father remaining alone in the living-room.

'I have work to do in the study,' he smiled at her as if he had read her thoughts, and they left the living-room together.

Cara followed her mother up the stairs, but on the top landing Lilian paused and placed a detaining hand on Cara's arm.

'John Curtis was here yesterday afternoon while your father was out.' Cara felt herself go cold as she waited for her mother to continue. 'He wanted to know about you and Vince, and he asked the oddest questions.'

'What sort of questions?' Cara prompted, holding her breath.

'Well, he wanted to know from me what I know about Vince, and he also wanted to know why we allowed you to marry a man like Vince Steiner.'

Cara was fuming inwardly with annoyance, but outwardly she looked calm as she met her mother's perturbed glance. 'What did you tell him?' Lilian gestured expressively with her hands. 'I told him I didn't know more about Vince than anyone else knew, and your father and I couldn't very well stand in your way once you had made your choice.'

If John was going to go snooping around, then Cara could foresee trouble ahead, but she kept this to herself. 'Was that all John wanted to know?'

'He asked if I thought that you loved Vince, and I told him that I presumed you did or you wouldn't have married him, but then,' Lilian laughed lightly, 'you have always been good at hiding your feelings.'

'John and I have been friends for a long time,' Cara tried to reassure her mother. 'He wasn't here when Vince and I were married, and it's only natural that he would be concerned for me.'

Lilian's features relaxed. 'I never thought of it that way.'

Cara felt disturbed by her mother's disclosure, but there was no sense in confronting John and making an issue of it, for it would merely increase his suspicion. She shrugged it off, and found comfort in spending the night in the room she knew so well. If she made the effort she could almost make herself believe that the past three weeks had been nothing but a bad dream, but that circle of gold on her ring finger was reality, however, and she could not escape the truth entirely. Neither could she escape the pain of knowing that she loved a man for whom she ought only to feel contempt.

Cara got into bed some time later and switched off the light, but she could not sleep. She toyed with the thought of taking a sedative, but she decided against it, knowing that she would wake up in the morning with a headache. The house was quiet, almost too quiet, and she found herself holding her breath as if she expected something to happen. Would Vince find her note, or would he go directly to Chantal's room without checking? Cara shifted about restlessly in bed in an attempt to shake off the pain and misery, and she went to sleep at last from sheer exhaustion.

She slept so soundly that she never heard her bedroom door opening and closing, and neither did she stir when the bedside light was snapped on. She was awakened only when a heavy hand descended on her shoulder to shake her, and she raised her heavy eyelids to find Vince standing next to her bed.

'Oh, you're home,' she muttered sleepily, turning over on to her other side when the light hurt her eyes, but the next instant she was wide awake to the fact that this was her parent's home and not Vince's. She shot up in bed, her eyes wide with fright as she clutched the covers about her. 'What are you doing here?' she demanded, her voice lowered and husky.

'I've come to take you home,' Vince informed her brusquely, and she wrenched her eyes from the blazing anger in his glance to consult the bedside clock.

'Do you realise it's almost midnight?' she whispered incredulously.

'Get up and get dressed,' he commanded harshly, his big hands clenching and unclenching at his sides as if he were tempted to wrap them about her throat, and a shiver of fear raced along her spine.

'Are you crazy?' she croaked valiantly, but she regretted it the next instant when Vince leaned over her with his hands pressing into the bed on either side of her body.

'Why did you tell your parents I was away for the weekend?' he demanded in a low, harsh voice, and she could almost feel the anger vibrating through the length and breadth of him.

'I never told them anything of the sort,' she denied indignantly, but she could not ignore that faint stab of guilt. 'When I asked if I could stay the night they took it for granted that you were away.'

'And you never bothered to tell them that it wasn't so?'

She looked away from his cold, piercing eyes and, to her dismay, felt the sting of tears behind her eyelids. 'Oh, go away and leave me in peace.'

Hard fingers gripped her chin and turned her face up to his to meet the searing fury of his glance. 'You're going to sleep in *my* house, in *my* bed, and nowhere else! Do I make myself clear?'

'And while I'm sleeping in *your* bed, Vince, where will you be sleeping?' she demanded with a burst of courage which had emerged from her deep misery. 'In Chantal's bed?'

His mouth tightened into a thin, cruel line which frightened her, and in one sweeping movement he pulled the covers aside and jerked her out of bed so that she stood trembling on the carpet in front of him. His hands were biting savagely into her bare shoulders, and she had to catch her quivering lip between her teeth to prevent herself from crying out.

'Get dressed!' he hissed through his clenched teeth, releasing her at last, and she stood for a moment examining the red marks against her skin which she knew would be ugly bruises in the morning.

'You hurt me,' she complained.

'You're lucky I haven't thrashed you,' he countered

bitingly, bringing his face so close to hers that she could see the stubble of beard along his jaw. 'Now get dressed!'

To protest would be futile; one look at his face told her so, and she turned meekly towards the wardrobe to haul out her clothes. She took off her nightie and pulled on her slacks and her sweater. She could feel Vince's eyes boring into her, but she was suddenly too tired to care.

'How did you get into the house?' she dared to question him while she packed the rest of her things into the overnight bag.

'Your father was still in his study.'

Cara picked up her brush to pull it through her hair a few times, then she paused in alarm, and swung round to face Vince. 'What am I going to tell him?'

A cynical smile played about Vince's mouth. 'I have already made the necessary excuses for you.'

'Oh?' Her alarm spiralled. 'May I know what you said?'

'I told him that I have brought home with me a female guest and, naturally, it would not look right if we spent the night alone in the house without you.'

Cara stared at him in momentary silence, her glance taking in the arrogant tilt of his head, and that hint of triumph in the cynical smile curving his mouth. He had lied to her father, but his lie had been laced so strongly with the truth that she could almost admire him, and quite suddenly she had a strange desire to laugh a little hysterically.

'How very clever of you,' she murmured when she had succeeded in controlling herself, and she turned from him to thrust her brush into her bag.

'Is this all?' Vince asked abruptly, taking her overnight bag from her when she had zipped it shut.

'Yes.'

'Right.' His hand gripped her elbow as if he suspected she might try to escape from him. 'Let's go.'

CHAPTER SEVEN

VINCE's face was expressionless when he ushered Cara down into the hall. Her father was still in his study, she could see the strip of light beneath the door, but she did not blame him for choosing not to confront Vince again.

Cara shivered when the cold night air hit her tired body moments later, and Vince's hand was like a steel strap beneath her elbow when he propelled her towards his Mercedes.

'What about my car?' she questioned him agitatedly.

'I'll send Jackson to collect that rattle-trap of yours in the morning,' he said abruptly, opening the door on the passenger side of the Mercedes and bundling a very indignant Cara into the front seat.

How dare he call her Mini a rattle-trap! The desire to defend her faithful little car stormed through her, but she had time for rational thought while Vince walked around the bonnet of the car to the driver's side, and she had to admit to herself, albeit reluctantly, that he had spoken the truth. Her second-hand Mini was actually no more than a rattle-trap, and if she had not thought so herself, then she would have driven out to the cottage that afternoon instead of reacting to the crazy impulse to spend the night with her parents.

Vince did not speak while he was driving, and in the dashboard light the harsh angles and planes of his features did not encourage conversation. She sat quietly with her hands clenched in her lap, and tried to understand why he had gone to the trouble of fetching her, but she was nowhere close to a reasonable explanation when they arrived at his home.

He carried her bag into the silent house, his hand once again clamped beneath her elbow and making her feel like a prisoner. He switched off the lights in the hall before they climbed the stairs, and Cara suddenly nursed a crazy fear of coming face to face with Chantal. She could not bear it if she had to confront that woman now; she was too vulnerable, and it would be too humiliating. There was no sign of light beneath Chantal's door, but Cara did not relax entirely until she was in the comparative safety of the master bedroom.

Vince dumped her bag on the floor at the foot of the bed, but he made no attempt to leave the room. He stood with his hands on his hips, his arrogant head lowered a fraction, and a brooding intensity in the way he observed her. It made her feel jittery, and her hand was shaking when she raised it to flick her hair back over her shoulder. What did he want? Why was he looking at her so oddly? Cara knew a sudden desire to escape when she thought of spending another night like the one before, and her insides knotted with tension and anger.

'I presume Chantal is keeping her bed warm for you, so there is no need for you to hang around, Vince,' she broke the awful silence between them, and it was as if she had put a match to a fuse.

'Let's get one thing straight!' he exploded savagely, lessening the distance between them in one long stride. 'I went to Chantal's room last night to teach you a lesson, but I never touched her in the way you think.'

Relief washed over Cara like a jet of cool water on a scorching summer's day, but an element of doubt lingered stubbornly in her mind, and when she thought of how she had suffered she erupted furiously. 'You surely don't expect me to believe that, do you?'

His jaw hardened, and she could not be sure, but it seemed as if he had gone a shade paler about the mouth. 'I'm not that much of a bastard that I'll make love to another woman with my wife's knowledge.'

'And what about today?' she asked scornfully, turning away from him. 'You had all day alone with her to make up for last night.'

'That's true.'

She winced inwardly, but she had to know. 'Did you?'

Cara felt him come up behind her, and she trembled inwardly even though he did not touch her. 'Would it matter to you if I did?'

Her throat tightened and tears filled her eyes. It had been foolish of her to question him, and she was amazed now at her own temerity. 'I'm tired,' she explained, and this was the truth. Her limbs felt like lead, and her head was pounding. 'I'm simply too tired to continue with this postmortem.'

'You haven't answered my question.' His hands on her shoulders turned her relentlessly to face him, and there was no time to hide the stinging moisture in her eyes. He studied her closely for some time before a faint smile touched his mouth. 'I think your tears are giving me the answer I required.'

Oh, lord! What was he thinking? Has he guessed that she has been stupid enough to fall in love with him?

'I'm tired, that's all,' she tried to explain away her tears, but she did not sound very convincing to her own ears.

'I know, Cara, *liebchen*,' he murmured softly, running his fingers through her hair, and she ached suddenly for him to hold her in his arms, but he did nothing of the kind. He helped her to undress instead, and put her to bed as if she were a child.

Cara was all at once too tired to care. She had barely slept the night before, and the hours of mental agony were beginning to take their toll. Through heavy-lidded eyes she watched Vince pull his sweater off over his head, and she did not avert her glance when his hands went to the buckle of his belt. The muscles rippled in his arms and across his hair-roughened chest. His stomach was firm and flat, his hips slim, and, for the first time, she found joy in studying his superb physique. His skin was tanned, and the naked maleness of him sent little tremors of awareness racing through her which she tried desperately to still. He knew she was watching him, but he did not turn away from her, and a curious smile was playing about his mouth when he finally got into bed beside her and switched off the bedside light.

She lay there in the darkness, conscious of Vince's body within touching distance of her own, and aware of a longing so intense that her tiredness evaporated like mist before the sun. If only Vince would touch her. If only he would do *something* instead of lying there so quietly and uncaringly as if he was totally unaware of her presence. Oh, God, she had never dreamed that she would ever reach the stage where she would actually want him to make love to her. She had never felt so desperate, nor so wanton, and pride suddenly took a back seat.

'Vince. . . .' Dear heaven, did her voice have to sound so wobbly, so uncertain, and so distinctly pleading? 'I can't sleep.'

He did not reply at once, and her body grew tense with shame. What was happening to her? Did loving someone strip one so completely of one's pride and self-respect?

'Neither can I,' Vince admitted when the silence had

stretched almost to breaking point, and she breathed an inward sigh of relief.

Be careful, she warned herself. *Don't make your feelings so obvious.* 'Would you like something to drink? Warm milk, perhaps?'

She wanted to laugh out loud at herself, but she controlled the desire swiftly when Vince asked mockingly, 'Do you think a glass of milk would help?'

He knows! a little voice screamed at the back of her mind. She was shamelessly doing everything except putting into words what she wanted, and Vince knew it. He knew exactly what she wanted, *damn him*!

'It might help,' she heard herself saying a little weakly.

'And then again, it might not,' he laughed throatily.

Cara felt that she could not stand this slow torture a moment longer, but, before she could say anything, he reached out and drew her close. Their bodies touched, fire meeting fire, and she was so overwhelmed by her feelings that she buried her face against his shoulder.

'Oh, Vince . . .' she whispered jerkily, and her lips parted eagerly beneath his when his mouth found hers in the darkness.

He made love to her that night with an unexpected tenderness, and her tired body felt rejuvenated as he sent her senses spinning towards undreamed of heights. She was giving herself for the first time with her mind as well as her body, and it was an experience that left her with a feeling of awe when they finally went to sleep with their arms still locked about each other.

Cara slept late the Sunday morning, and when she awoke she found herself alone in bed. Her immediate reaction was that of disappointment, but it swiftly changed to relief when she began to recall her own behaviour the night before. She would have time to pull herself together before having to face Vince, and she would have time to think of a way to eliminate the impression she must have given him.

She bathed quickly and chose to wear a brown woollen skirt with an amber-coloured knitted sweater. She was in a brown and yellow mood today, and furious with herself. What on earth had possessed her to make her feelings so obvious last night.

Vince and Chantal were standing out on the sunlit terrace when Cara went down to breakfast. She hesitated, tempted for a moment to hide rather than face them, but she poured herself a cup of coffee and squared her shoulders bravely before she went out to join them. Their conversation ceased abruptly the moment Cara stepped out on to the terrace, and she had an awful suspicion that *she* had been the topic of conversation. Vince's eyes smiled into hers with that familiar mockery she was beginning to detest, and she was dismayed when she felt herself blushing to the roots of her hair. If she could have drowned in her cup of coffee she would have done so, and Chantal's tinkling laughter told Cara that those green eyes had not missed a thing.

'I would never have believed that your wife could still blush after three weeks of being married to you, Vince,' Chantal remarked slyly, linking her arm through his, and looking Cara up and down with a strange brightness in her eyes. 'If I didn't know you so well, Vince, I could almost have believed that last night was your wedding night.'

Cara had always prided herself on her coolness and rigid composure under any given circumstances, but her armour had slipped dangerously the moment she had stepped out on to the terrace, and now it was completely shattered. Her cheeks were burning, and she was quite incapable of doing anything about it.

'I find it quite enchanting when Cara blushes,' Vince laughed softly, his compelling glance drawing Cara's against her will, and her heart fluttered like a wild, caged bird against her ribs. 'It is one of the many things I find so attractive about her.'

Chantal's laughter, mocking and hateful, made Cara's anger rise like a volcano about to erupt, and flames darted from her eyes when she placed her untouched cup of coffee on the cane table and turned to face them.

'I'm pleased to know that I have been a source of amusement to you,' she spoke sharply. 'Life would be very dull indeed without something to laugh at, but having fun at someone else's expense is never in good taste.'

Cara turned on her heel and walked away from them, but not before she had seen the tightening of Vince's jaw. She had angered him, but at that precise moment she could not care less. She needed to cool off and regain her composure, she told herself as she strode fiercely into the garden.

The wooden summer house was shaded and the crimson bougainvillaea ranking over it offered her the privacy she needed. The silence there had a therapeutic effect on her, and she felt herself beginning to relax, but that feeling did not last long. A shadow fell across the sunlit, concrete floor, and she looked up to see Vince's tall frame blocking the entrance. His mouth was tight, and his eyes were cold, and she felt the underlying anger in him like a vibration being transmitted across the space between them.

'Go away and leave me alone,' she pleaded quietly, but he ignored her near desperate plea for solitude.

'You were unnecessarily touchy, Cara, and I'd like to know what the hell is the matter with you?' he demanded harshly, and his voice was like the lash of a whip across bare, sensitive flesh. 'Can't you laugh at yourself occasionally, or don't you have a sense of humour?'

This was not the moment to vent her frustration and anger on him, but anger was her only defence at that moment. 'My sense of humour is still intact, thank you, but there has been nothing very amusing about being forced into this marriage, and I can find nothing humorous in being mocked by your mistress—past or otherwise.'

'Careful, *liebchen*,' he warned, a flash of derision in his eyes. 'You're beginning to sound like a jealous wife.'

'Oh, I *hate* you!'

She raised her clenched fists, intending to strike at his chest in her fury, but he caught her wrists smartly, and jerked her up against his hard body. Imprisoned and helpless in his arms, his mouth descended on hers to silence her protests, and a fire was kindled deep down inside of her that left her trembling and breathless when at last he released her. She stood swaying in front of him, dizzy with the force of her emotions, and she felt too weak to protest when he placed a steadying arm about her waist.

'I think we won't talk of hating,' he mocked her and, when she would have pulled away from him, his arm tightened about her. 'Chantal wants to leave and is waiting to say goodbye.'

That was the best news he could have given Cara, and her antagonism melted away almost at once.

Chantal was leaning elegantly against the bonnet of her red Porsche when they approached the house, and her chic black-and-white striped outfit gave her an air of sophistication which one seldom found outside a fashion magazine. There was fire in her hair, and a fire of a different nature in her eyes when they met Vince's.

'Yesterday was a day to remember, Vince, and I thank you for it.' Her smile was provocative and the hand she placed against Vince's cheek was suggesting a familiarity that rankled. 'We have always been good for each other, haven't we?'

'Always,' Vince smiled, taking her wrist between his strong fingers and kissing her palm while Cara stiffened with displeasure at this display of intimacy. 'Drive carefully,' Vince warned.

'I shall,' Chantal laughed enchantingly, sliding gracefully behind the wheel of her Porsche and turning the key in the ignition. The engine purred to life, and only then did Chantal acknowledge Cara's existence. 'Take good care of him for me, Cara.'

The red Porsche swept down the drive, but Cara was now almost blind with a new kind of fury. *Take good care of him for me.* For how long? Until this senseless marriage was ended and Chantal could take him back? Cara bristled with anger, and then something else Chantal had said came to mind. *We have always been good for each other, haven't we?*

Good for each other in what way? Cara wondered. The physical sense? Pain, like the talons of an eagle, clawed at her heart, and Cara wondered how much more she would have to endure before she would have to walk away from this marriage perpetrated for the sake of revenge.

'Where do you think you're going?'

A heavy hand stopped Cara when she reached the terrace steps, and she did not miss that hint of anger in Vince's voice, but she was equally angry when she shrugged off his hand and spoke without turning. 'I have brought home a book from the libary which I want to read.'

Vince followed her up the steps, but his fingers

snaked about her wrist before she could enter the house and, with that uncanny ability to read her mind, he said: 'I think you misunderstood Chantal's statement.'

'I don't think I did,' she contradicted, controlling her features before she turned to face him, but she was unprepared for the disconcerting intensity of his gaze. It seemed to penetrate her defences and inject a weakness into her which she could ill afford at that moment.

'Last night, Cara. . . .'

'Last night *you* misunderstood,' she interrupted him hastily, and her voice was surprisingly cool. 'I was tired, and tiredness often plays nasty tricks on one.'

He smiled twistedly. 'It made you want me so much that you couldn't sleep?'

'Surely you also have moments when you are vulnerable,' she argued, dragging her wrist free of his grasp. 'Women are irresistibly attracted to you, and I admit that I am no exception. You are also a very experienced lover, and I am not going to deny that I did want you last night, but I was vulnerable and susceptible.'

'And it was no more than that?' he demanded mockingly.

'If part of your desire for revenge entails making me fall in love with you, Vince, than I must ask you to remember what I told you on our wedding night,' she reminded him in a desperate attempt to lead him away from the truth. 'I said then that I could never love you, and I meant it.'

'If I remember correctly, I then warned you that loving me would never do,' he reminded her in turn of the things they had said to each other on that hateful might, and his narrowed eyes observed her intently while he lit a cigarette. 'What, I wonder, has given you the impression that I have any desire for love to enter into our relationship?'

She studied him warily, and she was beginning to hurt unbearably. 'What are you hoping for, then?'

'An honest understanding,' he smiled faintly, blowing smoke from his nostrils and looking more like the devil she knew him to be. 'The kind of understanding where we can say how we feel without the other one thinking we are beginning to harbour thoughts of undying love.'

'Have you never been in love?'

Silly question, she chided herself. Vince had a cold slab of concerte where his heart ought to be, and his reply confirmed this.

'No, I have never been in love, and I don't ever intend to be,' he said in a clipped voice, and it had the power to intensify her agony. 'What about you?'

Cara lowered her lashes to veil her feelings. 'Loving someone only brings pain.'

He was silent for a moment and she could not bear to look at him when he asked: 'You have had this experience?'

'Yes.' There was no harm in admitting the truth, and it need not lead him to discovering that she was speaking about her feelings for him.

'I take it you are not referring to John Curtis?' he probed cynically, and her heart was beginning to pound uncomfortably.

'No, I'm not.'

'Would you like to talk about it?'

'No!' she cried anxiously.

'Cara!' His hand gripped her arm when she would have fled from him in fright. 'Do we have an understanding?'

The wild, frightened beat of her heart subsided. 'An honest, no-holds-barred understanding?'

'That's it.'

Her eyes met his; guardedly at first, and then with unwavering and growing confidence. 'Very well.'

'Good,' he said abruptly and, leaving her out there on the terrace, he walked into the house.

Cara heard his footsteps disappearing in the direction of the study, and she shook her head as if to rid herself of the confusion in her mind. Vince Steiner was quite the strangest man she had ever known. One minute she imagined that she understood him, and the next he left her feeling totally confused. She sighed audibly as she went inside to fetch the book she had brought from the library, and she told herself that there was no sense in trying to understand the man who would be her husband for a year and no more.

It was an unusual Sunday; it drifted by in a relaxed fashion which was quite contrary to weekends past, and Vince was surprisingly pleasant company when he had succeeded in coaxing her away from her interesting historical novel. He was not behaving at all to pattern, and she felt bemused and bewildered that evening as she changed for dinner. Was it possible that he had been trying to flirt with her?

Cara thrust aside this thought and told herself not to be ridiculous. She flung open the cupboard doors and chose a wine-red dress with flaring skirt because she knew she looked good in it and, instead of tying her hair up into its usual knot, she brushed it vigorously and left it loose for a change.

She felt relaxed, but when she walked into the living-room her body tensed at the sight of Vince standing in front of the fireplace. A cigarette was dangling from his fingers, and his brooding glance settled on her when she walked towards the crackling log fire to warm her hands. She could not decide at that moment which she preferred; his mocking, often cynical remarks, or this silent appraisal that made her intensely aware of that aura of sensuality which surrounded him. He had the ability to touch her with a glance, and he was doing so now with a determination that made her body tingle. He turned from her to pour a sherry for both of them, and Cara subsided weakly into a chair. She arranged the wide skirt of her dress about her knees, and she did so with unnecesary concentration, but there was a part of her which was still intensely aware of Vince.

There was confidence in every movement he made, and his clothes were always expensively and impeccably tailored to accommodate his tall, well-proportioned body. She stared at his broad, formidable back in the dark blue jacket, and his gold wristwatch flashed in the light when he returned the bottle of sherry to the cupboard. Cara lowered her eyes hastily before he turned towards her, and she did not raise them again until his suede shoes came into her line of vision. His grey slacks stretched tightly across his muscled thighs, and their fingers touched inevitably when she took the glass from him. It was like fire darts racing up the length of her arm, making her want to snatch her hand away, but she clamped down on her jumpy nerves, and succeeded in bringing the glass to her lips without spilling a drop of sherry.

'Dinner is served, Master,' Jackson announced, and Cara welcomed his intrusion at that awkward moment.

'Thank you, Jackson,' Vince nodded, and his hand rested lightly beneath Cara's elbow when they crossed the hall and entered the dining-room.

Their conversation was oddly stilted throughout dinner, but it was a welcome change from those brooding glances which disturbed her so. The kitchen staff had excelled themselves, but Cara was reminded of her first night in that house. Then, just as now, she had been unaware of what she had eaten, or whether she had eaten at all. On that first occasion she had been terrified at the thought of what lay ahead of her, but this time she was simply too disturbed by Vince's ice-grey eyes that never gave her a moment's peace to enjoy her food.

Jackson served cofee in the living-room, and then they were left completely alone. Cara sat down, but Vince once again took up his brooding stance in front of the fireplace. She might still have been able to cope with the inexplicable silence between them, but his eyes were now glittering with a sensual fire when his glance trailed over her, and her heart began to pound with a force that threatened to choke off the air to her lungs.

'Don't look at me like that, Vince,' she protested, her voice unnaturally sharp with the effort to hide the fact that he had unnerved her.

'I can remember the first time I saw you.' His eyes lingered a moment longer on the agitated rise and fall of her breasts before his glance met hers, and a faint smile curved his often cruel mouth. 'It was at an exhibition of local art in the Town Hall, and you were wearing an ivory dress trimmed wth lace. You had your hair done up in a Grecian style, and I remember thinking that you were as cold and aloof as the statue you were admiring.'

Cara could remember that evening only too well. She had felt his compelling glance drawing hers like a magnet from across the length of the room. She had wanted to look away again, but even at a distance he had wielded a powerful force, and he had held her glance captive for several interminable seconds before his eyes had trailed over her feminine curves with an insolence that had sent a fire surging into her pale cheeks.

She felt a little faint with the memory of it, but her voice was etched with sarcasm when she said: 'You obviously have a good memory.'

'I can also recall that I found you most intriguing, and I couldn't take my eyes off you.'

The latter was true. She could remember vividly that, no matter where she had turned, his eyes had followed her relentlessly, and because of this she had left before she had seen all the exhibits.

'I can recall thinking that you were deliberately trying to make me feel uncomfortable,' she retorted with a spurt of sudden anger.

'A spark was ignited when our eyes met,' he continued as if she had not spoken, and she wondered frantically if this was a part of that honest understanding he had spoken of earlier that day. 'Did you feel it too, *liebchen*?'

'Yes,' she snapped defensively. 'It was a spark of antagonism.'

'It was more than that, and you know it,' he contradicted mockingly, placing his empty cup on the mantelshelf and lighting a cigarette. 'I knew then that I had to have you, but it was the knowledge that you were David Lloyd's daughter that made me decide to wait.' Smoke jetted from his nostrils, and his eyes were narrowed to unfathomable slits while he observed her. 'I had a feeling you would come in useful some day, and I was right.'

Cara did not have to be reminded that she was being used, but somehow it hurt her more now than ever before, and she lowered her long dark lashes to hide her pain. 'You accused my father and I of using people, but aren't you doing exactly the same?'

'I set a goal for myself when I was twenty,' he said with a harshness that made her wince inwardly, 'and I am not ashamed to say that I have used people in the past to get where I am today.'

'And do you consider that something to be proud of?' she asked scathingly, anger giving her the courage to raise her glance to his.

His eyes burned into hers for a moment, then he frowned down at the tip of his cigarette and shrugged carelessly. 'I am not always proud of the things I have done, but there has been a purpose behind everything I have done.'

'The purpose of it all being that your ultimate success finally put you in a position to repay my father in kind for something he did to you long ago?' She was not quite sure whether she ought to admire his patience and determination, or whether she ought to despise it. 'Is that what you're saying?'

'Yes, that is what I'm saying.'

He was being honest; that was something she ought to be grateful for, but it did not alleviate the pain which was growing inside her like a cancer. If he explained, then she might uncover something to afford her a spark of understanding, and it was with this thought in mind that she said: 'Don't you want to tell me what happened?'

'No!' The word was as decisive as his action when he flung his half-smoked cigarette into the grate, and her heart leapt into her throat when he stepped forward to remove her untouched cup of coffee from her hands. 'We have talked enough, I think.'

The glint in his eyes should have warned her what to expect, but she was totally unprepared when he lifted her bodily out of the chair and carried her from the living-room. His arms were hard about her waist and behind her knees, and there was no escape from their steely grip.

'Put me down, Vince,' she protested when he crossed the hall, but she knew from the set of his jaw that her plea was as futile as if she had asked him to cease his vendetta against her father.

He mounted the stairs as if he were carrying no weight at all, and he did not put her down until they had reached the bedroom, but he did not release her entirely. His warm mouth against hers was like a potent drug sapping her energy, and she was only barely conscious of what was happening. With no confining coil in her hair, he worked his fingers through it repeatedly as if he loved the feel of it, and her scalp tingled pleasantly. He undressed her slowly, but deftly, pausing often to arouse her with sensual little kisses against her smooth, responsive skin and, when he had cast aside the last flimsy garment, her legs seemed to give way beneath her. She despised herself for loving him and wanting him the way she did but her mouth moved eagerly beneath his when he lifted her in his arms and lowered her gently on to the bed.

Cara's trembling body was pale in the moonlight that filtered in through the window, and she was aching for his touch when he released her to shed his own clothes. She shivered without the warmth of his arms about her, but he was beside her in an instant, his arms cradling her against him until the heat of his rock-hard body flowed into hers. His lips teased hers, their sensual warmth exciting her when he trailed a tantalising path down to her breast, and she locked her fingers in his hair as a moan of pleasure burst from her lips. He was using her, but she did not care, and this was the last coherent thought that tripped through her mind before the intimacy of his caresses shut out everything except the ecstasy of those spiralling sensations he aroused.

'You are so beautiful, *liebchen*, you put fire in a

man's blood,' he murmured close to her ear, his voice vibrant with the extent of his desire, and sanity returned to her for a brief moment.

'Sometimes I—I wish I had never—never met you,' she whispered unsteadily, but even as she spoke her body yielded to the demand of his.

'Our meeting was inevitable, Cara,' he laughed softly and exultantly. 'I am tempted to say it was written in the stars.'

At any other time she might have been capable of conjuring up several stinging replies to his statement, but the passionate fusion of their bodies shut out everything except that vortex of shattering sensations from which she did not want to escape.

Words of love hovered perilously on her lips, but later, when she went to sleep in Vince's arms, she thanked God that they had never been spoken. To confess her love to Vince would give him yet another savage weapon to use against her, and in the end her father would suffer equally as much.

CHAPTER EIGHT

THE weeks slipped by, bringing them ever closer to the time when they would know who had acquired the contract for the second steel plant, and the tension of waiting and not knowing was almost unbearable. Cara's marriage to Vince continued on the new understanding that they could say what they wished without fearing their remarks would be interpreted as a commitment of any kind. It allowed for a more relaxed relationship, but for Cara not a very satisfying one. Vince could, at times, be attentive and almost gentle, but Cara was always aware of that ruthless quality in his nature, and that fiery anger which never lurked far from the surface of his often casual manner.

Cara was becoming increasingly concerned about her father. On the last few occasions she had seen him he had not looked well, and the pressure of waiting was beginning to take its toll. She tried to be optimistic about the future, telling herself that her father's chances of procuring that contract were as good as Vince's, but that discomfiting element of doubt was always there. Vince was clever and influential, and he was in the habit of getting what he wanted.

Despite Cara's attempts at adopting a positive attitude she could not deny the heightening of tension as the time of waiting drew to a close, but she was forced to shift her problems temporarily into the background when John Curtis walked into the library unexpectedly one morning. She had not seen him since that unfortunate encounter shortly after her marriage,

and she was still rather annoyed with him for
approaching her mother with his probing questions, but
she chose to forget the latter as she linked her arm with
his and took him through to her office.

'You're just in time for tea,' she said, and the usual
pleasantries passed between them while she poured and
passed a cup to him across her desk, but she sensed
rather sadly that the easy relationship between them
was crumbling. John was tense and awkward, and she
was beginning to feel the same.

'I behaved rather badly the last time we met, and I've
come to apologise,' he broke the uneasy silence which
was beginning to develop between them, and his green
eyes did not quite meet hers.

'There is no need to apologise, John,' she assured him
hastily. 'We have been friends for many years, and I can
understand how you must have felt when you
discovered I was married to Vince without so much as a
hint to you.'

'I was angry and disappointed,' he confessed, and a
tiny little frown settled between Cara's winged brows.

'I can understand your anger at returning from your
holiday to find that I had married a man I had once
declared that I detested, but——' She paused and bit
her lip in confusion. 'Why were you disappointed?'

'Disappointed is a mild word to what I actually felt,'
he laughed ruefully, staring down into his cup. 'I had
always imagined that we would get married one day,
and I was so sure you felt the same that I foolishly
waited too long to propose.'

'Oh, John. . . .' She faltered helplessly and was forced
to admit that Vince had been correct in his assumption,
but that did not make it easier for her to face up to the
situation. 'I . . . I don't know what to say.'

'Don't say anything, Cara,' John waved aside her

remark with a gesture she knew so well, but the hurt lay undisguised in his eyes even though he smiled. 'I'd still like to be your friend, and I'll be around if you should ever need me.'

Their friendship had meant a great deal to Cara, and knowing that she had hurt him brought a lump to her throat which she had difficulty in swallowing down before she could find her voice sufficiently to say, 'I wouldn't want to lose your friendship. It has meant a lot to me in the past, and I know it will in the future.'

'I don't know if you're interested,' he changed the subject when they had had their tea, 'but I've heard a rumour that the directors of the steel company are in the process of deciding which tender to accept for the new steel plant, and their decision should be made known at the end of this week. I believe both your father and your husband have tendered for it, and that must put you in a bit of a fix when it comes to deciding where to give your support.'

That was putting it mildly, Cara thought, her tension spiralling once again. She had expected a decision to be made soon, but she had not exactly known when, and she had been too afraid to ask.

'My father needs this contract very badly, and I sincerely pray that he gets it,' she confided.

'I should have known,' John laughed, his eyes regaining some of their familiar warmth. 'You have always given your whole-hearted support to the losers of this world, and you will never change.'

His remark had not been made unkindly, but Cara felt herself stiffen with annoyance. 'My father is not a loser.'

'Perhaps not,' John shrugged, 'but he could do with a sizeable amount of cash in the bank, and that is common knowledge in Murrayville.'

Cara felt disturbed that John should know more than she had known until Vince and her father had enlightened her two months ago. She had been so busy living her own life that she had not seen what was going on under her very nose, and it angered her now to think that she had been so unobservant.

'I can't deny that my father needs the money, because it happenes to be true,' she conceded at length. 'His company, or what is left of it, is practically on the rocks.'

'Is your mother aware of what is going on?' he unknowingly placed a finger on the very reason why she had married Vince.

'No, she doesn't know. It would merely upset her, and my father and I are hoping, of course, that it won't be necessary to enlighten her.' Her hands were clenched so tightly in her lap that they actually ached, and she tried consciously to relax the tension which was bunching up the muscles in her body. 'My father's problems will be solved if he gets this contract.'

'And if he doesn't get it?'

Cara went cold at the thought. 'He *must* get it.'

'It's as important as that, is it?'

John studied her intently, and there was no need for her to reply to his query. He could see the answer in the tightness about her soft mouth, and in the flicker of panic which momentarily darkened her eyes.

Cara sat like a frozen statue behind her desk for some minutes after John had left. She could not thrust aside that gnawing fear that her father might not get the contract he so desperately needed, and it was this fear that made her decide to go and talk to her father during her lunch hour.

Her mother was out at a luncheon party, Cara discovered when she arrived at the house, and she was relieved that she could talk privately with her father without the fear of her mother walking in on their conversation.

'Is it true that the directors of the steel company are busy deciding on which tender to accept?' she asked without preamble, seating herself on the corner of the desk close to her father's chair.

'It's true,' David Lloyd confirmed, pushing his fingers uncharacteristically through his greying hair. 'And Friday is the deadline.'

Cara studied her father closely, taking in the unhealthy pallor of his skin, and that strange restlessness which made him run his fingers through his hair at short intervals. He did not look very sure of himself, but she had to ask: 'Do you feel confident?'

'No construction engineer can feel confident when the competition is as powerful as the Steiner Company,' he smiled twistedly, and her eyes followed his hands as he reached for his cigarettes.

'When was the last time you went to the doctor for a check-up?'

'I'm not ill.'

'Whenever I see you your hands are shaking,' she told him bluntly, her glance shifting to the tiny beads of moisture forming on his forehead, 'and it's unnatural to perspire the way you are doing in this cold weather.'

'Stop fussing, Cara,' he protested agitatedly, lighting his cigarette and blowing the smoke forcibly towards the ceiling.

'You're also smoking too much,' she accused when she saw the nicotine stains on his fingers.

'Did you come here to lecture me?' he demanded angrily, and the harshness of his voice was something she was unaccustomed to.

'Despite everything, Dad, I happen to care about

you, and because I care I am concerned for you,' she said quietly. 'Go and see the doctor . . . please?'

He frowned and moved his shoulders jerkily as if to shake off the suggestion. 'I'll make an appointment for next week.'

'Why wait until next week?' she demanded with a forced calmness. 'Why not see him tomorrow?'

'I'm too busy,' David Lloyd argued, gesturing a little wildly with his hands, and drawing deeply on his cigarette as if he gained strength from the nicotine and tar.

'Busy with what?' she persisted anxiously. 'Busy sitting here worrying about whether you're going to get that contract with the steel company?'

'For God's sake, Cara!' he exploded, slamming his fist on to the desk and getting to his feet at the same time. 'I'll see the doctor next week, and let's just leave it at that.'

She had never seen her father this agitated before, and it frightened her. The veins stood out like roadmaps against his temples, and the beads of perspiration on his forehead were becoming more noticeable. His hands shook violently when he raised his cigarette to his lips, and his shoulders were hunched when he walked jerkily towards the French windows.

'All right, Dad, I won't force the issue, but there is something I want you to know,' she told him as she slid off the desk and picked up her handbag. 'You are more important to me than the necessity to keep this house, or large sums of money in the bank and, if Mother knew the truth, I am sure she would agree with me.'

She did not expect a reply from him, and neither did she wait for one. She walked out of his study and closed the door behind her, but she was blinded by tears when she reached her Mini. If anything happened to her father she would never forgive Vince, she decided fiercely, and a new kind of fear had her in its vice-like clutches.

Cara soaked herself in a hot bath before dinner that evening in an attempt to ease the tension from her body, but nothing seemed to help. She sat through dinner with Vince, barely conscious of what she was eating, and lost in the frightening thoughts racing through her mind. What if her father cracked and died under the pressure as Siegfried Steiner had done? *Oh, God, no!* It did not bear thinking about!

Jackson cleared away the dinner things and they took their coffee through to the lounge where the fire crackled in the grate. Vince buried himself behind the newspaper, and Cara tried to read the book she had brought home with her, but the words danced before her eyes without real meaning. She tried desperately to concentrate, but each time she did so her father's pale, anxious features leapt up at her from the printed pages.

'You've been very quiet this evening,' Vince finally remarked, folding up the newspaper and drinking the remainder of his coffee.

'I'm worried about my father,' she confessed, hoping, against her better judgment, to strike a chord of sympathy in Vince. 'The strain is too much for him.'

'Is that so?' Vince smiled, and that flicker of triumph in his steel-grey eyes made her realise once again the hopelessness of the situation. Vince was hard to the core of his being, and compassion was an emotion he would never know.

'You don't need this contract, Vince,' she pleaded desperately, putting her book aside and kneeling at his feet in an unconsciously pleading attitude. 'Won't you consider withdrawing your tender and giving my father a chance?'

It was like battering herself against a steel door. She knew that she would never succeed in so much as denting it, but she was desperate enough to go on trying.

'And what will I recieve in return for such a supreme sacrifice?'

His eyes were narrowed and intent upon her pale, pinched face as she kneeled on the floor in front of him, and her heart was suddenly pounding in her ears. At any other time she might have told Vince to go to the devil, but for her father's sake she knew that she had to cast aside her pride and make a supreme sacrifice of her own.

'I'll stay married to you for as long as you want, I'll have children for you, and I'll slave for you ... oh, God!' The enormity of what she was offering made her bury her quivering face in her hands for a moment, then she let them fall into her lap and gestured pleadingly. 'I'll do *anything*,' she ended on a husky note.

The silence in the room was intense, and when a log crackled in the grate Cara reacted to the sound with a violent start.

'Your offer doesn't appeal to me in the slightest,' Vince's harsh voice grated across her raw nerves. 'Now, if you will excuse me, I have a few telephone calls to make.'

He rose to his feet abruptly, and there was a look of such utter contempt on his face that she wanted to shrivel up and die as he walked out of the living-room.

Cara sat there, too numb to do anything while her eyes filled with hot tears of humiliation. She had only herself to blame for the stinging bitterness of his rejection, but it was a chance she had been forced to take. She had cast aside her pride to save her parents, and Vince had rejected her cruelly. She had failed; not only in herself, but in her attempt to help her father, and at that precise moment she could not decide which hurt the most.

The flames leapt crazily in the grate, and Cara felt their heat against her cheek when she wiped away her tears with trembling fingers. She stared into the fire, seeing there her hopes being burnt to ashes along with her fragile dreams as if she had literally cast herself into the flames. If she had imagined that Vince might learn to care for her in some way, then she knew now how mistaken she had been. The only thing he cared about was to avenge his father's death, and nothing, it seemed, would deter him from the goal he had set for himself.

Cara parked her Mini in the driveway on the Friday evening, and she had clutched the steering wheel so tightly that her fingers felt numb when she got out of the car. The tension had been building up in her since early that morning, and it had now reached the point where she felt as stiff as if she had run a marathon. She had been too afraid to call her father to find out if he had heard anything, and every time the telephone had rung on her desk she had jumped as if a whip had been cracked beside her.

Jackson opened the door for her and took her coat and, before he could say anything, a flash of crimson in the living-room had caught Cara's attention.

'Harriet!' she exclaimed, entering the spacious room and walking towards the flaxen-haired woman who stood warming herself by the fire. 'What an unexpected surprise.'

Grey eyes met Cara's curiously. 'Vince didn't tell you I would be coming for the weekend?'

'No,' Cara frowned, biting her lip to steady the sudden quiver in it. 'It must have slipped his mind.'

'Like hell it did!' Harriet exploded in typical Steiner fashion, her features resembling Vince's at that moment. 'Vince telephoned me on Wednesday evening and practically instructed me to be here this afternoon, or else.'

Cara felt the chill of ice sliding through her veins as she said lamely, 'I—I wonder why.'

'I've a pretty shrewd idea,' Harriet snapped, her glance holding Cara's, 'And I think you have as well.'

Fear clawed at Cara, but the sound of a car coming up the drive saved her from making Harriet aware of her feelings. 'I think I hear Vince's car now,' she said unnecessarily, thrusting her hands into the pockets of her skirt to hide the fact that they were shaking.

They did not have long to wait. Vince's long, lithe strides brought him swiftly into the house, and Cara's treacherous heart bounced wildly at the sight of him. His dark, striped suit had been tailored to accentuate the steely strength of his muscled body, and Cara trembled inwardly. Her glance was riveted to his tanned, rugged features with the sun-bleached hair which the breeze had whipped across his broad forehead. His eyes glittered strangely as if with an inner excitement, and Cara felt the tension coiled tightly like a spring inside her.

'Ah, Harriet, I'm glad to see you have arrived safely,' he smiled that twisted smile when he brushed his lips in a brief kiss against Harriet's cheek, then he turned towards Cara, and she felt his cool mouth brush against her warm cheek in much the same manner it did Harriet's. 'You look a little tired, *liebchen*,' he remarked with mocking concern. 'Have you been working too hard today?'

'Not more than most days,' she replied stiffly, aware of Harriet leaning a casual arm along the mantelshelf while she observed them together.

'I think I have the perfect tonic for all of us,' Vince announced, walking towards the cabinet and producing a chilled bottle of champagne.

'Champagne?' Harriet's eyebrows rose cynically as they watched him remove the wrapper and ease the cork from the neck of the bottle until it shot out with a loud bang that made Cara flinch. 'What are we celebrating, Vince?'

Cara stood as if she had been nailed to the floor. Her skin felt heated and damp, but her insides were slowly turning to ice.

'We are celebrating my success, Harriet,' Vince announced, his deep-throated voice triumphant. 'My tender has been accepted for the new steel plant.'

The sound of clinking glasses jarred Cara's nerves, and there was a soaring in her head that made her fear that her tight control would snap if she did not hang on to it desperately. Her thoughts flew at once to her father, and she knew a sudden desperate need to be with him at that moment.

'Excuse me,' she forced the words past her frozen lips and, snatching up her car keys, she headed towards the door.

'*Cara!*' Vince's authoritative voice halted her abruptly in her stride. 'You will come back here.'

Harriet detached herself from the mantelshelf. 'Vince, don't you think you are——'

'Don't interfere, Harriet,' he silenced his sister, but his cold grey eyes never left Cara's white face. 'Come here, Cara,' he ordered.

His voice was quiet, but ominous, and Cara knew that she dared not disobey him. She walked towards him unwillingly on legs that felt like jelly and, when she paused a little distance from him, she raised her chin to say coldly, 'I'm here.'

Vince passed a glass of champagne to Harriet and raised his own, then he turned to Cara and gestured towards the remaining glass on the low table close to them. 'Pick up your glass and drink to my success.'

A storm of protests rose in her throat, but they died there when she looked into the glacier coldness of his eyes. She knew that she had to obey him, but she knew also that she could not pick up that glass. 'What you're expecting of me is totally monstrous.'

'Do as you're told.'

'I would be displaying a disloyalty to my father if I drank to your success,' she protested helplessly, wishing he could know how he was tearing her in two.

'Surely as your husband, I am entitled to your loyalty?' he demanded derisively, and an icy anger emerged from her helplessness.

'You have done nothing to deserve it,' she snapped.

'You will nevertheless do as you're told,' he countered with a calm, hateful arrogance. 'Raise your glass, and drink to my success.'

Their eyes locked in silent battle for interminable seconds before Cara surrendered to his superior strength. She picked up the glass of champagne, her fingers curling about the stem, and she caught a glimpse of sympathy in Harriet's eyes when she straightened. That unexpected sign of sympathy was almost Cara's undoing, but she blinked back the tears, and raised her glass with a touch of defiance in the set of her chin.

'I shan't drink to your success, Vince, but I'll drink to the sincere wish that your desire for revenge will at last be satisfied so that you may rid yourself of the hatred which is slowly destroying you.' She raised the glass to her lips, and swallowed down a mouthful of the bubbling liquid. 'Now, if you will excuse me, I'd like to go and see my father,' she added, returning her glass to the table.

'You will do nothing of the kind,' Vince stopped her once again before she reached the door, but this time her anger was an uncontrollable force that shuddered through the length of her slender body.

'You have succeeded in grinding my father into the dust beneath your heel, and there is nothing I can do about it, but don't expect me to live with your hatred,' she spat out the words furiously. 'I'm going to see my father; I have a right to see him, and you need not fear that I shan't be back to act as hostess at your dinner table this evening.'

Cara turned on her heel and walked out of the room with Vince's eyes boring into her back. She had a horrible feeling that he might make an attempt to prevent her from leaving, but this time he let her go, and five minutes later she was driving as fast as she could towards her parent's home on the other side of town.

Fear had taken second place to fury for a few moments, but, as her fury subsided, her fear returned like a cold gust of wind blowing up against her. *No construction engineer can feel confident when the competition is as powerful as the Steiner Company*, she recalled her father's words when she had called on him not two days ago, and she could not help thinking that he must have known he did not stand a chance against Vince. Something told her that Vince had been equally aware of this, and she was convinced that part of his triumph at that moment was because he knew this would be the final blow; the final humiliation which would crush her father completely. There was no possibility now of the loan ever being repaid unless her father sold everything he possessed, and that was the only degrading solution.

Cara drew in an anguished breath, but it sounded more like a sob. She loved Vince, but at that moment she hated him for what he had done to her father, and she was almost too afraid to think of what she would find when she arrived at her parent's home.

'Cara, I'm so glad you came,' her mother greeted her anxiously in the hall, and the strained, anxious look on her mother's face was a painful, uncommon sight to Cara. 'Your father's tender was not accepted for the new steel plant.'

'I know, Mother.' Cara spoke with a calmness she had dredged up from somewhere. 'Where is he now?'

'In his study.' Lilian pointed towards the panelled door in the hall, then her hand gripped Cara's arm, and there was a look of uncertainty in her eyes when they met Cara's. 'Is there something I—I don't know about?' Lilian asked, and she was almost pleading.

Cara looked away, unable to sustain her mother's glance. 'If you know that Dad has lost that contract, then you know everything.'

'I'm not a fool, you know,' her mother said, and there was a hint of exasperation in her voice. 'I've known for some time that your father has been anxious and troubled about something, but he refuses to tell me what it is, and I'm also terribly worried about his health.'

'That makes two of us,' Cara thought, but aloud she said: 'May I go through and see him?'

'Yes, my dear,' her mother agreed at once, 'and please see if you can find out anything.'

'Oh, God, how tired I am of this deceit,' Cara thought as she turned towards the study door. She knocked once, but when there was no response, she opened the door and went inside. David Lloyd was sitting with his elbows resting on his desk, and his head buried in his hands. He looked dejected and totally beaten, and Cara's heart contracted with pity and compassion as she closed the door behind her.

'Dad ...' she began, not quite knowing what to say as she approached his desk hesitantly, and only then did he look up.

A tremor of shock raced through her at the pasty colour of his skin and, as if he needed to do something with his shaking hands, he lit a cigarette and drew the smoke almost savagely into his lungs.

'I suppose you have heard the news,' he grunted, raising glazed, empty eyes to hers.

'Yes, I have.' She searched for something to say; something to reassure him, but she could think of nothing except a rather lame, 'I'm sorry.'

'Not half as sorry as I am,' he laughed with a cynical harshness she had never heard before, and there was something rather frightening about it.

He looked ill; *terribly* ill, and it was doubly painful knowing that it was Vince who had done this to him. 'What are you going to do?' she asked, seating herself on the corner of the desk close to him.

He puffed agitatedly on his cigarette, surrounding himself as well as Cara in a cloud of unsavoury smoke. 'I shall have to declare myself insolvent and start again somewhere.'

The thought of her father having to start all over again at his age was something she could not envisage for a moment. 'You will have to sell this house.'

'I know that,' he said abruptly, drawing hard on his

cigarette and surrounding himself with yet another smoke screen.

'Have you told Mother?' she asked, but it was a silly question to which she already knew the answer.

'Not yet.'

'She suspects something, she has told me so, and there's no longer any sense in putting it off,' she warned him, recalling her conversation with her mother in the hall.

'I know, I know,' her father muttered, pushing a shaky hand through his hair, then an odd little smile suddenly twisted his mouth. 'I imagine Steiner must be very pleased with himself?'

Steiner. An odd mixture of bitterness and guilt was locked up in the use of Vince's surname, and she could not fully understand it, but she imagined it had to be something like the love–hate feeling she had for Vince at that moment.

'I wish you would tell me what actually happened between you and Vince to lead to this destruction of everything you have worked for,' she broached the subject which had been puzzling her over the past months.

'It's a long story, Cara, and I'm too tired to even think straight at the moment,' her father side-stepped the issue once again. 'All I know is that I have ten months to scrape together the amount owing to Vince, and I know I'm not going to meet that deadline unless I sell everything.'

'I could ask you not to come to a hasty decision, but I know it is absolutely futile to sit back and hope for a miracle,' Cara said logically.

'God knows, I could do with a few miracles,' her father grunted, crushing his cigarette into the over-full ashtray and lighting another.

Cara was on the point of saying something about his recent habit of chain-smoking, but she stopped herself in time. This was not the moment for a lecture she decided, as she placed a comforting hand on his shoulder. 'I wish there was something I could do.'

'You've done enough already,' he said, raising his hand to grip hers briefly, and she knew that he was referring to her marriage to Vince. 'Go home to your husband, Cara, and your mother and I will sort out this mess together.'

Cara was reluctant to leave him, but she knew that if she stayed she would not be able to help him in any constructive way. She was powerless to do anything to prevent her father's downfall, and knowing this made her feel like lashing out at anything and everything that came her way.

'Cara?' her mother's voice halted her when she walked quickly across the hall, and Cara felt a swift rise of panic within her at the thought of the questions her mother was going to ask. It was important that she knew the truth, but it was for her father to tell her mother in his own good time.

'I must hurry, Mother,' she said quickly, planting a kiss on her mother's soft, perfumed cheek. 'Vince hates having dinner delayed, and I have already stayed too long.'

That, in itself, was not a lie. Vince would not want dinner to be delayed on that specific evening, but Cara was disgusted with herself for using that as an excuse to escape from her mother. She felt like a coward, which she was not, but she could not shake off that feeling. Along with her father she had practised deceit in hiding the truth from her mother, and the only thing that appeased her was the knowledge that her father was the best candidate when it came to a confession. He knew the complete truth, which had, to date, been withheld from Cara, and she dared not intervene at this stage.

CHAPTER NINE

THE atmosphere at the dinner table that evening was highly explosive, but Cara was positive that it was not entirely due to the incident which had occurred between Vince and herself before she had gone to see her father. Judging from the stabbing glances which passed between Vince and Harriet, they had had a furious argument after Cara's departure, and their differences had obviously not been resolved.

Harriet excused herself immediately after dinner to go up to her room, and one glance at Vince's thunderous expression made Cara follow suit a few minutes later.

It was a cold, dark night, and Cara bathed quickly before going to bed, but she could not sleep. She was anxious about her father, and she had to admit that she was also concerned for Vince. His desire for revenge was alienating him from his sister, the only person for whom, Cara felt sure, he cared. A pang of envy shot through her, but she suppressed it at once. Harriet was his sister, and she had a right to Vince's affection, but Cara could not help wishing that a fraction of that affection could have been directed at herself.

Cara was still awake two hours later when Vince came into the bedroom. Her hair lay in disarray across the pillow, and her eyes were troubled when she glanced up at him, but she forgot her problems for a brief moment to study him. His hair was damp after his shower. It lay in a disorderly fashion across his forehead, and she knew from experience that his muscled frame had nothing on beneath that brown towelling robe which was tied so carelessly about his waist. His masculinity was as potent as a drug, and her pulse quickened against her will when he approached her side of the bed and stood looking down at her with a hint of derision in his eyes.

'It's a pleasant change to find you lying awake instead of pretending to be asleep,' he mocked her openly. 'Is it that your concern for your father has overshadowed your distaste for my presence in your bed?'

She sat up abruptly, letting her hair fall forward to veil her flushed face. 'My father is not well, Vince.'

'So Lloyd is beginning to feel the pinch, is he?' Vince snarled, then he laughed harshly, and the sound of his laughter made her body tense. 'Now he will begin to know how my father felt, and that's exactly what I have wanted to achieve.'

Cara winced inwardly and observed him through lowered lashes while he lit a cigarette and drew hard on it. There was anger in every movement he made, and it was etched deeply in his harsh profile when he turned from her. It frightened her to see him like this, and it hurt to know that there was nothing she could do about it.

'Why do you hate my father so much?' she asked, her hands clutching nervously at the sheet. 'What did he do?'

'Why don't you ask him,' came the harsh reply, and Cara's eyes followed him in despair as he walked around to his side of the bed.

'I'm asking *you*, Vince.'

Steel-grey eyes met hers beneath frowning, fair brows, and his jaw was so taut that the muscles jutted out on either side. She fully expected him to brush aside

her query once again, but a tired look flashed across his
rugged face, and he sat down heavily on the bed. He
studied the tip of his cigarette for endless seconds as if
he were trying to decide on something, then he drew
hard on it once more, and crushed the remainder into
the ashtray on the bedside cupboard.

'My father used to hire himself out as a sub-
contractor to larger companies,' he enlightened her at
last on this painful subject, and she steeled herself in
preparation for what she was about to hear. 'Eighteen
years ago Lloyd hired my father to assist in the erection
of the building which now houses the municipal
employees. My father studied the plans and, when the
material was being delivered to the sight, he told Lloyd
that the steel reinforcement was insufficient for a
building of that size and structure. Lloyd wouldn't
listen to him. He insisted that the new quality steel
would be quite sufficient in quantity and strength, and
my father reluctantly bowed to his superior knowledge.'
Vince's mouth twisted with derision as he met her
steady glance. 'The building had barely reached the
second floor level when a section of it collapsed under
pressure. Two of my father's men were killed, and
several were injured.'

'Oh, no!' the words were torn from Cara, and her
hands covered her mouth as the horror of the incident
hit her, but Vince was too engrossed in his thoughts and
painful memories to hear her.

'Lloyd had a clever lawyer, and when the matter went
to court he accused my father unjustly of negligence
and several other things besides. My father was a
simple, trusting man, but it was a case of his word
against the written proof your father had in his
possession that sufficient steel had been ordered,' Vince
continued, and the bitterness in his voice was almost

too much for her to bear. 'My father got off lightly when they took his past record into consideration, but the stigma of that incident clung to him and, as a result, no company would hire him. With his pride and his dignity shattered, and with his integrity continually questioned, my father gave up on life and shot himself.'

Cara went cold as if someone had poured a bucket of chilled water over her. She could understand, at last, the reason for Vince's desire for revenge, but what she could neither understand, not accept was the implication that her father had almost deliberately ruined Siegfried Steiner's career as well as his reputation. Something was dreadfully wrong, but she would not know what it was until she had spoken to her father and had persuaded him to relate his side of the incident to her.

'I was twenty at the time,' she heard Vince saying, 'and I was studying engineering, but the money in the bank was dwindling, and I had to find myself a job while I continued my studies. Harriet was fourteen at the time. She had ambitions of becoming a doctor, and I was determined that she would not be disappointed. 'I sold everything we possessed here in Murrayville, and rented a cheap flat in Johannesburg for myself and my sister. I attended lectures during the day, and at night I did anything from a steward at a restaurant to a road-house attendant. I needed every cent I could lay my hands on, and I spent most of my weekends doing private building and repairs jobs. Harriet also had her fair share of those hard times. She cooked and cleaned, and somehow managed to fit in time to attend to her studies.' His features twisted savagely and he lit another cigarette, blowing the smoke out of his nostrils like a furious animal. 'When I finally completed my studies I knew exactly what I was going to do. I worked for a while to save up enough money, and in the end I started my own company. I started small, but I literally clawed my way to the top of my profession. I was moving in the right circles and, when I heard rumours of the steel plant which was being planned for Murrayville, I knew that the moment I had been waiting for had arrived. The most important objective in my life was to break Lloyd as he had broken my father, and now I have succeeded.'

Cara sat there staring at him, her eyes brimming with tears, and a numbness spreading through her body. She had never been confronted with such bitterness before, and she wanted to reach out to comfort him, but she suppressed the desire knowing that, to Vince, it might seem as if she was offering herself once again in an attempt to save her father.

Her hand went out hesitantly to touch his arm, and she could feel the muscles grow taut beneath the towelling material of his robe. 'Vince, I'm sorry about your father, but are you sure there wasn't some mistake?'

'There was no mistake,' he snarled, brushing off her hand as if it were something obnoxious, and his eyes stabbed at her with a blazing fury in their depths. 'Your father was trying to make a packet out of the deal by using the absolute minimum of material and, if we hadn't all been so ignorant at the time, we could have fought and won the case.'

She lowered her gaze dismally and blinked away her tears. 'If what you say is true, then I can't blame you for feeling the way you do, but——'

'But *what*?' he rapped out the query when she faltered.

'The things you have said about my father don't ring true somehow,' she confessed, stretching her loyalty to the maximum. 'He may be weak in some ways, but I

have always known him to be totally sincere, and
painfully honest in business.'

'You have obviously been mistaken.'

Cara shook her head and gestured helplessly. 'There
must be some dreadful misunderstanding.'

'There was no misunderstanding,' he contradicted
harshly, getting to his feet and pacing the floor as if to
rid himself of a burst of excess energy. 'Lloyd accused
my father publicly of negligence, and in the building
trade that amounts to the death sentence.'

The numbness began to leave her, but it made way
for a new kind of torment. She was being torn in two by
her loyalty to her father, and her loyalty to Vince which
was born of a love he had no need of.

'I'm sorry about what happened, Vince, but to
continue this vendetta against my father isn't going to
bring *yours* back, or right the wrong that was done,' she
pointed out.

'I know what I'm doing.'

'No, you don't!' She was angry now and, unconcerned
about how much of her he could see through her flimsy
night attire, she leapt out of bed and clutched at the
sleeve of his robe to halt his furious pacing. 'You're
being eaten up inside by hatred and the desire for
revenge, and you can't live like that,' she argued
desperately for *his* sake as well as her father's.

'I don't need a lecture from you about how I should
and should not live my life,' he replied with a savagery
that made her back a pace away from him. 'You want
me to drop everything, and you want me to give your
father a chance, but you can forget it. If Lloyd had
once—just *once*—paused to give my father a chance
when the odds were against him, then I might have
considered giving *him* a chance now, but under the
circumstances your father doesn't deserve it.'

Her tawny eyes, wide and pleading, met the chilling onslaught of his glance. She had a premonition of something yet to come, and she gestured in despair as she croaked: '*Please*, Vince.'

'No way!' he snarled, walking away from her to crush the remainder of his cigarette into the ashtray. 'Forget it!'

He loosened the belt about his waist and shed his robe and, for a brief moment, she had a glimpse of his perfectly proportioned body before he got into bed and pulled the covers over him. He turned on to his side and switched off the light, and Cara stood there like a statue for several seconds before she realised that she was shivering with the cold.

She crawled into bed beside him and switched off her own light. She felt defeated. She had listened to everything he had told her, and she had tentatively tried to reason with him, but she should have known that nothing would dissuade him from what he was doing to her father. She lay staring into the darkness, her eyes filling with hot tears, and she had never felt more desolate in her life. They were sharing a bed for the first time without touching each other, and she could not decide at that moment which was worse; the vendetta he was carrying out against her father, or this invisible barrier which had suddenly risen between them?

She wanted to touch him; she wanted to feel his hard male body against her own, and she wanted the strength of his arms about her to assuage some of the fears storming through her, but the barrier between them was totally impregnable. She was being ridiculous and irrational, but the hot tears slid down her cheeks on to her pillow. She wept silently for all the things which could have been. If only Siegfried Steiner had not taken his own life. If only her father had not had a part in that fatal act. If only . . .! There were so many that she could not count them on her fingers, but she went on counting them over and over until she drifted into oblivion from sheer exhaustion.

Cara awoke during the night to find Vince lying with a heavy arm draped across her waist. She knew he had not touched her consciously, but she derived a certain comfort from it, and she drifted at last into a sound sleep.

Cara started the Saturday morning with a feeling of uneasiness which she could not shake off. It lingered on through that cold, bleak morning, and the atmosphere in the house merely intensified that premonition that something was about to happen. She went for a stroll in the garden when the sun burst through the clouds after lunch, and she walked about restlessly, lost in thought and oblivious of her immediate surroundings. There was a certain beauty even in the starkness of winter, but Cara was unaware of it. A rose bush, sheltered from the first winter frost by the widepsread branches of an evergreen shrub, was bearing what would most likely be the last roses of that season, and their crimson petals provided that rather dreary section of the garden with a vivid splash of colour.

She did not see the roses; she saw only the dry leaves and twigs like a carpet beneath her feet, and the naked branches of the trees reaching up to the sky. Everything appeared to be dead, or in the process of dying, and that was exactly how Cara felt at that moment. She had been dying slowly since she had made the disovery that she was in love with Vince. He could never love her; he could never love *anyone*. There was room only for revenge in his heart, and that revenge was directed at the only other man Cara cared for deeply. She ought to hate Vince for what he was doing to her father, but she could not. Perhaps it was her misguided notion that, beneath his harsh exterior, there lurked a man who had once laughed often, and a man who could care very deeply if only he would allow himself to do so.

'Cara?' Harriet spoke directly behind her and, startled, she spun round almost irritably, but her irritation vanished when she glimpsed a plea in those eyes which were so very much like Vince's. 'May I walk with you?' Harriet asked hesitantly.

'If you wish,' Cara shrugged indifferently.

She had no desire for company at that moment, but the garden did not belong to her, and Harriet could walk where she pleased.

'I imagine you must dislike me almost as much as you dislike Vince at this moment,' Harriet remarked after they had strolled along in silence for several seconds, and Cara felt a little shiver of shock race through her.

'I don't dislike you, and I don't——' She bit her lips and gestured a little helplessly while she fought back the tears which seemed to leap so readily to her eyes. 'I don't dislike Vince, but I—I wish I knew of a way to ease this terrible desire for revenge he carries about with him,' she explained at length.

'The only thing which will ease his desire for revenge, I'm afraid, is to see your father completely shattered,' Harriet sighed, and she drew Cara into the summer house. They seated themselves on the wooden bench, and they were silent for some time before Harriet continued to speak. 'He wasn't always like this, Cara. He used to be fun, and gentle and caring, but our father's death hit him hard. He worked day and night most of the time to put me through school as well as university, and in the process he became the hard, unfeeling man he is today. Eight years ago he started the Steiner Engineering and Construction Company. He started with nothing, and it has taken sheer steely grit to build the company up to what it is today. He has made quite a few enemies in the process, and there are people who believe that to know him is to fear him, but I'm convinced that deep down inside of him he is still the good and caring brother I always knew.'

Harriet was not telling Cara something she did not know. She was, unknowingly, confirming part of what Vince had told Cara the night before, but Harriet was relating the past without the bitterness which had been so evident in Vince.

'I can only hope that hard outer crust will crack one day to release the old Vince,' Harriet concluded at length, and Cara silently echoed that wish.

She glanced briefly at Harriet and caught a glimpse of something in those grey eyes that made her feel uneasy. It was almost as if Harriet was pleading with her, and this awakened Cara's curiosity.

'What are you trying to tell me, Harriet?'

'I think you have the ability to bring about that change in Vince,' she said unexpectedly. 'I pride myself on being a good judge of character, and I detect in you that certain warmth, compassion and understanding that Vince needs so much at this moment.'

Cara stared at Harriet for a moment without knowing quite what to say, but it was despair that finally dictated the words that spilled from her lips. 'You are forgetting, perhaps, that I am David Lloyd's daughter.'

'All the more reason why I feel you are the one to heal the wounds of the past,' Harriet argued, but Cara could not forget the look on Vince's face that day at the cottage when she had questioned him about whether she was to be punished along with her father.

'You are David Lloyd's daughter, are you not,' he had replied scornfully, and Cara could not imagine that he would ever see her in any other light.

Jackson brought their conversation to an end by appearing at the entrance to the summerhouse, and he bowed respectfully towards Cara. 'Telephone for you, Madam.'

Cara felt a cold hand clutching at her heart as she thanked him and excused herself from Harriet. Every instinct within her was hammering out a message that put wings on her feet as she ran from the garden into the house, and she was breathless when she reached the telephone in the hall and snatched up the receiver.

'Hello, Cara Steiner speaking.'

'Cara!' Lilian Lloyd's voice was like a choked cry for help. 'It's your father!'

Those icy fingers clutching Cara's heart was now chilling the blood in her veins. 'What has happened?'

'He collapsed early this morning, and the doctor has him under sedation in the hospital,' her mother explained, and Cara's fear gave way to a white-hot rage.

'Where are you now?' she rapped out the question.

'I'm here at the hospital, and I——' There was silence for a moment while Lilian obviously tried to control her tears, then she added jerkily, 'I'm so worried, Cara.'

'I'll be there as soon as I can,' Cara assured her mother, and she slammed down the receiver a moment later.

Vince was to blame for this! She had seen her father crumbling under the pressure Vince had applied, and she would never forgive him if anything happened to her father. Never!

She stormed down the passage in an unaccustomed rage and burst into Vince's study to find him seated behind his desk with an open file in front of him.

He looked up, and those cold eyes raked her from head to foot in a way which would have made her cringe if she had not been so furious. 'I suggest you knock next time before entering my study.'

'My father is ill in hospital,' she informed him coldly, hoping against her better judgment to see some sign of remorse. 'He collapsed early this morning, and he's under sedation.'

His rugged features remained impassive except for a slight narrowing of his eyes. 'That's no excuse for bursting in here without knocking.'

'*Damn* you, Vince!' she exploded, her face white, and her tawny eyes sparkling with fury. 'Because your father is dead, do you want my father dead as well?'

'What your father does with his life is his choice entirely,' he replied with a callous indifference that stirred a reckless desire in her to lash out at him and, throwing caution to the wind, she did so.

'Your father had a choice as well, Vince, and he chose to shoot himself rather than face up to his problems.'

'Shut up!' he hissed savagely, his face dark with fury, and he rose to his feet with an abruptness that almost toppled his chair.

It was as if a sealed door had suddenly opened up in front of Cara. She had, unwittingly, found the right key, and she was staring into that forbidden chamber with its shadows and its pain. *I detect in you that certain warmth, compassion and understanding that Vince needs so much at this moment*, Harriet's words came unbidden to her mind. At any other time she might have been overcome with compassion, but at that precise moment she was consumed with anger and a terrible fear for her father's life. The truth had come to her at last as her glance clashed with Vince's during that brief, frightening silence.

'That's what is eating you up inside, isn't it?' she heard herself voicing her incredible discovery. 'You don't hate my father as much as you despise your own for not facing up to his problems and fighting back.' An awful whiteness seeped beneath the skin along his hard jaw, and his lips drew away from his teeth as if he was about to pass a cutting remark, but she did not give him the opportunity. 'Well, I'm damned if I'll let you drive my father to the point where he will want to put a gun to his head,' she slammed home her convictions. 'My father will fight back against whatever barriers you may wish to lay in his path, and my mother and I will be behind him all the way.'

Having said that, Cara stormed out of his study in much the same way she had entered it, and a few minutes later she was taxing her Mini to its very limit in order to reach the hospital as soon as possible. Her mind was in a turmoil of pain, anger and fear, and from deep within her a feeling of guilt was emerging which finally dominated every other emotion. How could she have allowed herself to fall in love with a man as cruel and callous as Vince Steiner? A part of her understood his actions and sympathised, but a part of her was totally repelled by what he was doing, and it resulted in an inward battle which was slowly tearing her apart.

The gravel spun beneath the Mini's wheels when she turned in at the hospital gate, and a few moments later she was walking almost at a running pace into the warm building. At the information desk she was told in which ward she would find her father, and she made her way quickly along the wide passages with the smell of disinfectant quivering in her nostrils.

'I'm so glad you could come.' Lilian Lloyd's eyes were red and puffy when Cara entered the private ward, and they embraced briefly before Cara's anxious glance shifted from her mother to the pale, still form of her father lying prostrate between the white sheets on the high hospital bed.

David Lloyd was lying so quietly that Cara could not be sure he was breathing, and fear slid its icy fingers about her heart once again. 'How is he?' she asked her mother in a husky voice.

'Still under sedation, as you can see,' Lilian subsided into the chair and dabbed at her moist eyes with a lace handkerchief. 'The doctor says that your father is suffering from complete nervous exhaustion.'

'Oh, God!' Cara lifted a shaky hand to her throat as she stared at her father, and her anger simmered inside her like a volcano threatening to erupt. Vince was to blame for this, and she knew now that she could no longer be a part of this relentless vendetta he was waging aginst her father. 'There is something you must know, Mother,' Cara said before she could change her mind.

'I know everything, my dear,' her mother forestalled her in a hushed voice. 'Your father confided in me this morning a short while before he collapsed.'

Cara's relief was so great that her legs actually began to shake beneath her, but then a new anxiety took possession of her. How much had her father told her mother?

'Did he tell you . . . everything?' she felt compelled to ask, but she ' ad difficulty in sustaining her mother's glance.

'I know why you married Vince Steiner,' Lilian confirmed Cara's worst fears in a voice that held a rebuke. 'I can appreciate the sacrifice you made, and the reasons for it, but I cannot condone your actions. Marriage is a serious business, Cara, and you have made a mockery of the vows you made.' Lilian's eyes filled with tears, and she gestured expressively. 'This is not the time to discuss your marriage, and I did not mean to lecture you.'

The lecture may not have been intended, but Cara felt chastised, and more than just a little ashamed. Her glance shifted to her father's white, drawn face, then back to her mother's tearful eyes, and her feeling of shame deserted her. If she could have spared them this moment of anxiety, then she would do it all over again, and pray that God would forgive her.

'Did Dad tell you what happened that time with Siegfried Steiner?' Cara changed the subject.

'Yes, he did.' Her mother's hand sought her father's and her fingers curled about his in a manner that seemed to seek as well as give comfort. 'The negligence was your father's. Siegfried Steiner had warned him that the steel would be insufficient, but your father had disputed this on the strength of the delivery note instead of taking the time to carry out a personal check. The company who had delivered the steel had also insisted at that time that they had sent the required amount, but a clever accountant finally found the error. There should have been a second delivery of steel to complete the order, but changes in staff had resulted in the company neglecting to despatch the remainder of the order.'

Cara digested this in silence. It confirmed what Vince had told her, but it still did not warrant his despicable actions . . . or did it?

'Why didn't Dad do something to restore Siegfried Steiner's reputation?' she put the question to her mother.

'It was too late to do that,' Lilian sighed sadly. 'Siegfried had already taken his own life, and his children had left Murrayville under a cloud and with no forwarding address. Your father tried to contact them, but without much success, and he finally decided to let the matter rest there.'

'I can't understand why Dad never tried to explain this to Vince when they eventually met.' Cara voiced her confused and troubled thoughts.

'Your father blamed himself for Siegfried's death,' her mother explained with tears in her eyes, 'and he was afraid that Vince would think he was using this information as an excuse to exonerate himself from that feeling of guilt he carried around with him.'

'So he chose to take whatever punishment Vince might decide to dish out,' Cara concluded a little cynically.

'And he involved you as well,' her mother added significantly, but Cara hastily directed the conversation away from the reason for her marriage to Vince.

'Did you and Dad have time to make any decisions about the future?'

'Yes, we did.' Lilian Lloyd eased her hand from her husband's and rose to her feet to walk across to the window, and she looked strangely old and defeated. 'If we sell up everything we will only just succeed in repaying the money owing to Vince, and we will start again with a clean slate. Losing the house and all we own is of no importance, but it is important that your father regains his strength and his vitality so that we can be together.'

Cara's throat tightened with renewed anxiety. Would the vendetta end here, or would Vince continue his relentless persecution? She thrust the thought from her and joined her mother beside the window. 'I'll stay here with you for as long as you need me.'

Lilian turned, and Cara saw a smile break through the tears in her mother's eyes. 'No, my dear, I'm feeling much better now that I have spoken to you, and there is no sense in both of us keeping a vigil beside your father's bed,' she said, dabbing at her eyes. 'Why don't you go home, and I'll call you as soon as there is news.'

Cara hesitated. 'Are you sure you will be all right?'

'I shall be quite happy to remain here at your father's side,' her mother assured her.

Cara glanced at her father's seemingly lifeless form and wished that there was something she could do to help, but the nurse who walked in a moment later appeared to be totally in command of the situation as she commenced her routine check.

Feeling superfluous, Cara embraced her mother briefly and left. She felt oddly as if she had transgressed beyond every other emotion except anger: anger against Vince for what he had done to her father, anger against Siegfried Steiner for leaving his son with a legacy of hatred and revenge, and anger against her father whose initial negligence eighteen years ago had instigated the entire disastrous affair.

CHAPTER TEN

CARA walked blindly along the hospital corridor and collided with a solid male frame when she turned a sharp corner. There was a familiarity in the touch of those steadying hands on her shoulders, and she knew that it was Vince before she looked up into those cold, shuttered eyes. She had thought that every scrap of feeling for Vince had deserted her, but she was alarmed to discover that, despite everything he had done, his nearness could still arouse that intense longing inside her. It was shattering to feel this way about someone who had done everything in his power to hurt her and those she loved, and she despised herself for it. An exclamation of disgust passed her lips as she gained the strength from somewhere to place her hands against his chest and push him away from her.

An unfathomable expression flickered in his eyes, and his mouth tightened grimly when he found himself confronted by the pent-up fury of her raised glance. 'How is your father?' he questioned her, an odd roughness in his usually smooth, deep-throated voice.

'He's still alive, if that's what you want to know,' she snapped.

His glance seemed to waver. From the inside pocket of his jacket he took out a slim gold cigarette case, but he realised in time where he was, and slipped the case back into his pocket. He appeared to be having difficulty in knowing what to do with his hands, and at any other time Cara might have found this significant, but she was too busy with her own turbulent thoughts to notice. She could still see her mother's eyes brimming with tears, and her father's white face against the pillow. It made her feel sick inside at the thought of what might happen if Vince continued with this vendetta, and a renewed bout of fear chilled the blood in her veins.

'Cara, I want to——' Vince began, but she cut in rudely, determined not to stand there listening to what he still had in mind for her father.

'I'm sure it will interest you to know that my parents have decided to sell everything. You will get your money, and they'll start again from scratch. 'I don't doubt that you're well aware of what it would entail for a man of my father's age to have to start again from the bottom, but I know he will succeed, and as for me. . . .' She paused to draw breath and, eyes flashing, she hissed her decision at him. 'I never want to see you again!'

She turned and fled from him, and he did not attempt to stop her. When she got into her Mini, however, her heart was pounding in her throat as if she had actually escaped pursuit. Her hands were shaking so much that she could barely insert the key in the ignition, then something snapped inside her and, burying her head in her arms, she burst into tears. Hot and salty, they slid down her cheeks and splashed on to the steering wheel, and several seconds elapsed before she was able to control herself sufficiently to drive home.

Home. Vince's house had never been *home* to her, and it never would be now. She had to leave him; she had no other choice. She ought to hate him, but instead she had fallen more deeply in love with him with each passing day, and she could not bear the thought of how she would cope with parting from him after a further ten months of marriage had elapsed.

The house was silent when Cara crossed the hall and

walked up the carpeted stairs. If she had not seen
Harriet's car in the driveway she would have thought
that she was the only one there. Her tears had long
since dried on her cheeks, and her jaw was set with
determination when she walked into her bedroom and
hauled a suitcase down out of the wall cupboard.

Cara worked swiftly and silently. She took her
clothes out of the cupboard with the slatted doors and
folded them neatly before she placed them into the
suitcase. Her thoughts drifted back reluctantly over the
past weeks, and she lived again through those
frightening days preceding her marriage to a man she
had not known. Marrying Vince had been the craziest
thing she had ever done in her life. He had bombarded
her into a decision with threats of ruination, and her
rational mind had become chaotic with fear. To give
her father more time to meet his commitment, and to
save the home her mother loved had been sufficient
motivation at the time, but now it all seemed so
ridiculous. If they had confided in her mother, then her
father would have been spared these agonising and
futile weeks of waiting, and Cara's marriage to Vince
would have been quite unnecessary. Lilian Lloyd had
proved at last that she was a woman of strength and
character, and Cara admired her mother more now
than she had ever done before.

The bedroom door opened suddenly, and Cara
looked up with a start to find Harriet framed in the
doorway. Her grey eyes, so like Vince's, darted from
Cara to the suitcase and back, then she pushed the door
slightly ajar, and approached the bed.

'You're not thinking of leaving Vince, are you?'
Harriet demanded with a hint of anxiety in her direct
gaze.

'I'm past the stage of thinking about it, Harriet,'

Cara explained, turning from Harriet to resume her packing.

'Don't you think you're being a little hasty? You could at least wait until Vince returns from the hospital, couldn't you?'

Cara hardened her heart against Harriet's plea, and folded a blue silk dress into the suitcase. 'I spoke to him when he arrived at the hospital to gloat, presumably, and I made it quite clear that I never wanted to see him again.'

'Please don't go yet, Cara,' Harriet pleaded. 'Give Vince an opportunity to explain.'

'To explain what?' Cara demanded cynically, brushing past Harriet as she walked towards the cupboard to remove a pile of lacy underwear from the shelf. 'I'm tired of being used as a pawn, and I refuse to sit back and do nothing about it while he pressurises my father into an early grave.' She turned from the cupboard to find that Harriet had taken up a stance between her and the suitcase, and there was a look of such determination in her eyes that Cara was momentarily startled, but she pulled herself together with equal determination. 'You're in my way, Harriet,' she said coldly.

Harriet gestured expressively with her hands, but she did not move out of the way. 'I can't let you go, Cara.'

Cara stared at her speculatively. Harriet had the advantage of being several centimetres taller, and Cara had to raise her chin to meet Harriet's grey gaze. They faced each other in silence as if they were sizing each other up to do battle, and if the situation had not been so painfully serious, then it might have been hilarious, for neither of them were aggressive by nature.

'I never thought that you of all people would want to prevent me from leaving,' Cara protested at length. 'I thought you would understand.'

'I understand a great deal more than you imagine, Cara,' Harriet's voice adopted a sternness which must have subdued many a difficult patient. 'You're in love with my brother, and you want to be loyal to him despite the circumstances of your marriage, but you're being torn in two by your attempts to be loyal to your father as well.'

Cara felt shattered. Harriet had sliced her open so deeply that her soul had been exposed, and Cara felt curiously numb for interminable seconds before the blood leapt through her veins again with a force that sent a hot wave of colour into her cheeks.

'Oh, lord!' she groaned, her pain a mental and physical thing, and her fear so real that it was almost tangible. 'If you have guessed my feelings, then Vince must have guessed as well, and all the more reason for me to leave now.'

'Vince is an astute and clever man, but in this instance he has been singularly blind,' Harriet laughed briefly with a touch of cynical amusement. 'He is convinced that he has succeeded only in making you hate him.'

Cara shook her head adamantly, and elbowed her way past Harriet to drop her pile of underwear into the suitcase. 'I've made up my mind, and I'm going . . . I *must*!'

'Cara. . . .'

Harriet's detaining hand gripped Cara's arm, but, before she could say more, an authoritative voice demanded sharply, 'What's going on here?'

A choked cry rose in Cara's throat as she spun round to face Vince, but the sound never passed her lips at the sight of his furious expression.

Cara was, for a moment, ridiculously afraid of what he might do, but she pulled herself together, and snapped: 'Isn't it obvious to you that I'm moving out?'

The deathly silence that followed made Cara's breathing sound laboured to her own ears, and Harriet faded insignificantly into the background as Cara withstood the steely onslaught of Vince's glance. There was something strange about him; something different, and Cara was still trying to decide what it was when he turned towards his sister.

'Leave us alone, please, Harriet,' he said abruptly, and Harriet obeyed him in silence, closing the door behind her as she left them alone in the room.

The atmosphere was incredibly tense, and the silence so prolonged that it began to gnaw away at Cara's nerves. Vince was standing a few paces away from her, his eyes almost feverishly bright in their sockets, and a strange paleness about his mouth. He looked ill and drawn, and she felt herself weaken, but only for a moment.

'I'm leaving you, Vince. I've made up my mind, and there is no way you can stop me,' she broke the silence between them, and it was as if the sound of her faintly husky voice triggered a spark of life in him.

'The agreement was, if I remember correctly, that our marriage would run the course of twelve months,' he reminded her as he observed her with glacier eyes once again.

'You have succeeded much sooner in your objective, and we both know that, if my father hadn't collapsed under the strain, you would have continued to hound him by placing stumbling blocks in his way to prevent him from having any success with his ventures,' she pointed out coldly. 'Under the present circumstances I feel there is no longer a purpose to our marriage and, quite frankly, I refuse to continue with it. My mother is aware of the truth, and we all know there is only one way my father can repay the loan he took from you.

They will have to sell everything they possess, and my mother is quite prepared to do that in order to help my father.'

A flash of unfathomable anger drove the palness from his face, and he breached the remaining gap between them in one long stride to tower over her. 'You're not going anywhere, Cara! You're staying right here!'

His attitude was menacing, but her anger rose sharply, and she raised her chin defiantly to meet his steely glance. 'I'm leaving, Vince, and there is no way you can stop me. Unless, of course, you chain me to the furniture, and you've stooped so low in the past that it wouldn't surprise me at all if you made use of such a barbaric method to keep me here.'

'*Damn you, Cara!*' His hands bit into her shoulders the one minute, and released her so abruptly the next that she staggered. He was breathing heavily, but he controlled himself with an effort that made the muscles jut out savagely along the side of his jaw. His eyes held hers with an unfathomable expression in their depths, then he looked away and lit a cigarette with hands that shook visibly. 'It might give you some satisfaction to know that you were right when you said I didn't hate your father as much as I despised my own for taking the easy way out instead of facing up to his problems and fighting back. I could have killed you for saying that. It shook me, but it made me think, and now I can only feel disgust for my own behaviour.' He gestured with the hand that held the cigarette as if to wipe out that incident when she had confronted him with the unvarnished truth as she had seen it. 'I've spoken with your mother, and as soon as I'm allowed to talk to your father I intend to make my peace with him.'

'You are ... what?' she asked incredulously, convinced that she could not have heard correctly.

'I'm going to make my peace with him,' Vince repeated with an unusual display of tolerance. 'I'm going to put him back into circulation by offering him a job as a sub-contractor with the erection of the new steel plant, and whether he accepts it or not will be up to him.'

Cara was mentally winded by this disclosure, but she remained sceptical. 'Did my mother explain to you about the discovery my father made some time after your father's death, and how my father tried to contact you without success?'

'Yes, she explained,' he said, turning to face her, and she wondered what lay hidden behind his shuttered eyes.

'The truth doesn't exactly exonerate my father, so I can't understand why you have decided to be so generous about it,' she remarked with a mixture of cynicism and suspicion in her voice.

'The truth may not exonerate him, Cara, but it makes a hell of a difference knowing he didn't deliberately ruin my father,' Vince explained, losing interest in his cigerette and crushing it into the ashtray.

Cara stared at him. She felt bewildered and not quite sure whether she ought to believe him, but she knew him well enough to know he seldom said anything he did not mean.

'Well, I'm glad you feel that way about it,' she said lamely, 'and I would like to thank you for the offer you are going to make my father, but that doesn't alter my decision to leave you.'

She turned away from him and walked towards the cupboard, but Vince moved with the swiftness of a jungle cat, and placed himself between her and the shelves. 'I'm afraid I'm not going to let you go, Cara.'

His mouth was drawn into a tight, angry line, but Cara was still fired with a deep-seated anger of her own. 'It's over, Vince, and I have no desire to continue with this senseless marriage.'

'The present situation does not alter our agreement.'

'Why not?' she demanded sarcastically. 'Does your generosity towards my father depend on whether you get your money's worth out of me?'

He went white about the mouth. 'Dammit, Cara, it isn't like that at all!'

'Isn't it?' Her tawny eyes were emitting sparks of fury. 'Why should I believe anything other than that?'

He raised his hand and she thought for a moment he was going to strike her, but instead he rubbed the back of his neck in an odd gesture of defeat. 'You're absolutely right, of course, when you say that our marriage has become rather pointless, and I realise now that it was barbaric of me to have forced you into it in the first place. I imagine the only decent thing I can do now is to tell you you're free to go, if that's what you want.'

That *was* what she had wanted. Vince had actually opened the proverbial door to the cage and he was setting her free, but his action filled her with grave misgivings. Incredible as it may seem, she was no longer so certain that she wanted to leave him. She thought of her father lying ill in hospital, and she suddenly found that she could not conjure up the slightest shred of anger against Vince, but it was too late now to change her mind. He was setting her free, and she knew that, whether it happened now or ten months later, the wrench was going to be agonisingly painful.'

She murmured something appropriate, and turned from him to hide the tears shimmering in her eyes as she reached blindly for a neat pile of blouses in the cupboard shelf.

She wished that he would go and leave her in peace, but he stood with his hands thrust into his pockets and his shoulders hunched while his eyes followed her broodingly as she moved back and forth between the cupboard and the open suitcase on the bed. His presence disturbed her intensely, and the prolonged silence unnerved her until she wanted to scream in the hope of relieving the awful tension.

'Where will you be staying?'

Cara's nerves jarred violently at the sound of his voice, and it took a moment to control the tremors racing through her before she could trust her voice. 'I'll stay with my mother until my father is out of hospital and on the mend, and then I want to concentrate on finding myself a job elsewhere.'

'You want to leave Murrayville?' he asked incredulously, his eyebrows meeting in a frown.

'I think that, under the circumstances, it would be the best thing to do, don't you?' she replied without looking at him, but he did not answer her, and he lapsed into yet another tense, lengthy silence that stretched her nerves to breaking point.

She could not get very much more into that one suitcase other than perhaps a sweater or two, and she was taking them out of the shelf when Vince's deep-throated voice disrupted the silence in the room.

'I have a few acquaintances in the literary world if you would like me to——'

'Thanks,' she interrupted him distastefully, 'but I would prefer to do things on my own, and preferably without assistance from you.'

'My flat is at your disposal if you're thinking of going to Johannesburg.'

'I wasn't necessarily thinking of going to Johannesburg,' she shied away from his offer. 'It will depend where I can get a suitable post, or where I might be needed.'

'You're needed here.'

That was an odd thing for Vince to say, but she shrugged it off, and packed her sweaters into the suitcase. 'My parents will need me for a while, I agree, but when my father——'

'*No!*' Vince barked savagely, and she narrowly missed having her fingers caught in the lid of the suitcase when he slammed it down. '*I* need you!'

How cruel he was to ignite a spark of hope where she knew there was none, and the pain of it pierced her like a heated blade. 'You don't need anyone, Vince.'

'Cara. . . .' He was interrupted by a knock on the bedroom door, and there was a flicker of annoyance in his eyes before he swung away from Cara. 'Come in!' he rapped out the authoritative command.

The door opened and Harriet's apologetic glance went from Cara to Vince. 'Mrs Lloyd has telephoned from the hospital to say that her husband is conscious and refuses to be sedated until he has seen you, Vince.'

He nodded curtly. 'I'll be on my way as soon as I've had a brief word with Cara.'

Harriet turned away in silence, closing the door behind her, and Cara was tempted to call her back, but that would have been silly. She was not afraid to be alone with Vince, was she?

'Please, Cara.' His hand gripped her shoulder with a certain urgency. 'I must make use of this opportunity while your father is conscious to speak with him, and I would appreciate it if you would wait here for me until I return.'

This was an earnest plea, not an arrogant command,

and the strangeness of it dispersed any desire she might have had to refuse. 'I'll wait,' she promised and, with a brief inclination of his head, Vince strode out of the room.

Cara stared at the door with the odd sensation that she had been left to dangle over the edge of a cliff. She had been relieved to hear that her father was conscious and coherent enough to ask to speak to Vince, but her mind veered back to the conversation she had had with Vince before Harriet had interrupted them.

'I need you,' he had said. Could he have meant it, or had he simply made use of differing tactics as a form of persuasion? Could he be that cruel? The obvious answer was in the affirmative, and Cara wrapped her arms about herself in an unconscious attempt to ease the pain that tore through her.

The afternoon had fled and the darkening sky heralded the commencement of another long winter's night. Cara sighed wearily and put her weight on the lid of the suitcase to fasten the catches. She would wait, but she knew that it would drive her crazy if she remained in that room a moment longer and, touching up her make-up hastily, she went downstairs.

Harriet was sitting in front of the fire in the living-room with a glass of sherry in her hand, and Cara poured a sherry for herself before she joined her there. Harriet staved off the silence by questioning Cara about her father, and Cara questioned her in turn for her medical opinion. It passed the time, and it also eased Cara's fears to know that there was no danger as long as her father rested up completely for a specified time.

Vince's car crunched up the drive shortly after six-thirty, and Harriet excused herself at once. 'I think Vince would prefer it if I left you alone to talk,' she explained when Cara tried to detain her.

The log fire crackled and Cara stood bathed in its glow, her hands fluttering nervously as she unnecessarily smoothed down her skirt. Why was she nervous? What was she afraid of? Vince walked into the living-room before she could find an appropriate answer to her frantic queries, and she could almost believe there was a look of relief in his eyes when they met hers across the room.

'Did you speak to my father?' she questioned him nervously when he closed the door.

'I did.'

'And?' she prompted, holding her breath.

'He has been kind enough to forgive me, and he has accepted my offer.' Their eyes met and held as he approached her, and his face looked grim. 'Won't you reconsider, Cara, and stay?'

'No!' She turned from him to hide the pain in her eyes. 'You agreed to let me go, and you can't change your mind now.'

'Cara. . . .' He swung her round to face him, and her glance sharpened when she felt a tremor in the hands gripping her shoulders. She saw that familiar mask crumbling, and his eyes were burning down into hers with a message in their depths which she was too afraid to grasp. A weakness invaded her limbs, and she felt herself swaying. 'My God, I can't let you go!' he groaned harshly, burying his face against her throat as he crushed her against his broad chest.

The bruising pressure of his arms was an ecstasy which she would have wanted to endure for life, but the agony of it finally forced her to stir against him in an attempt to ease the pressure on her ribs.

'Please, you—you're hurting me,' she gasped, and he released her at once.

'I'm sorry,' he grunted apologetically, but his feverish

eyes were still probing hers. 'I imagine you must hate me very much.'

Dear heaven! How could he talk of hate when that aching longing inside her was intensified with every beat of her heart? 'I don't hate you, Vince.'

Instead of appeasing him, her reply seemed to anger him, and he turned away from her abruptly. 'I would prefer your hatred to your indifference,' he said harshly over his shoulder.

'Indifference?' she echoed stupidly and somewhat startled.

'Yes, indifference!' he thundered, turning to pin her down with his stabbing gaze. 'You know,' he gestured with uncharacteristic wildness, 'it's that neutral state where you neither care one way or the other.'

Cara found herself staring at him as if she had never seen him before. His ruggedly handsome face looked tortured as if he was suffering the agonies of hell, and his feverish eyes pierced hers with a searching intensity that made her suspect he wanted to see deep down into the most secret corners of her soul. Why? Did he want the truth to mock and humiliate her?

'There have been many times when I have . . . hated you, but I have never felt . . . indifferent towards you,' she croaked hesitantly and with a great deal of wariness.

'What have you felt then?' he demanded and, when she had difficulty in finding an evasive answer, he took her by the shoulders and shook her almost savagely. 'For God's sake, Cara, I must know!'

'I—I can't tell you,' she stumbled over the words, and she was shaking so much that she was actually grateful for the agonising support of his large hands on her shoulders.

'Why can't you tell me?' he persisted hoarsely, his

eyes never leaving her face.

'Because I—I'm afraid,' she whispered, swallowing convulsively, and lowering her gaze to the pearly buttons on his blue shirt.

'Afraid?' he asked incredulously, then he laughed softly and somewhat exultantly as if something in her manner had told him her secret. 'What are you afraid of?' he asked, drawing her into his arms, and she sought refuge from his probing eyes by burying her flushed face against the smoothness of his suede jacket.

'I'm afraid you will laugh at me for being foolish enough to do the very thing you once warned me against,' the confession was torn from her in a smothered voice.

His arms tightened about her, drawing her more firmly against his hard, muscled body, and Cara found herself drifting somewhere between the heaven of his nearness, and the hell of lingering uncertainty. She felt his lips against her hair, her temple, and then they dipped lower to caress that very sensitive little spot behind her ear. An achingly sweet shiver of pleasure raced through her, and her arms circled his waist beneath his jacket as she pressed herself closer to him.

'Look at me, Cara,' he ordered softly, prizing her face out into the open with gentle fingers, and what she saw in his eyes made the blood pound with a joyous leap through her veins. '*Liebchen* ... I love you,' he murmured the words she had never imagined she would hear from his lips, and her happiness was so intense that her eyes filled with tears.

'I—I can't believe it,' she stammered helplessly.

'From the first moment I saw you I knew that I wanted you,' Vince continued, 'and for almost a year I accepted every damn invitation to some of the most ridiculous functions in the hope of seeing you there. I am not normally a patient man, Cara, but my desire for revenge was like a cancer in my soul that made me wait and, when the opportunity came to tie you to me, I used the foulest method of all to persuade you. I told myself that I would soon grow tired of you, but that day at the cottage—when we made love in front of the fire—I knew then that I loved you. I fought against it like the very devil; I decided never to touch you again, but every time we were together I found myself aching to hold you.' That haunted look was back in his eyes, and he crushed her against him with a fierceness which almost drove the breath from her body. 'Oh, my God, Cara, I can't let you go out of my life,' he groaned into her fragrant hair. 'I'm bitterly ashamed of what I did, and I want to make it up to you if you will let me.'

She tried to speak, but her throat was tight with tears of happiness. She swallowed and tried again, but she finally had to relinquish the effort in favour of a more primitive method of communication. She raised her eager lips to his and his tender kiss errupted swiftly into a passion which was not intended. Their bodies strained close, their lips and hands clinging, and they were both shaken and breathless when at last they drew apart.

'Tell me you will stay,' he ordered thickly, pulling the comb from her hair and running his fingers through the silken mass when it cascaded down to her shoulders.

'I'll stay, if that's what you want,' she murmured tremulously, finding pleasure in his touch.

'There has to be another reason for you to stay,' Vince insisted, sliding his hands down her back and up again beneath her soft woollen sweater to caress the soft skin at her waist.

'If I said that I—I loved you, would that be sufficient reason?' she asked, finding it difficult to think straight while her body responded deliriously to the feather-light caress of his fingers.

'Would you look at me and say that again?' He drew away from her a little when he said that, and her arms went up of their own volition to circle his strong neck.

'I love you,' she murmured, her tawny eyes glowing, and her lips aching for his, and somehow they were sharing one of the big easy chairs in front of the fire.

Vince murmured words of love in between passionate little kisses, his voice vibrant with an emotion she had never heard before, and it was a soothing balm for all the pain and anguish she had been forced to endure. Everything else faded temporarily into the background, but reality always intervened when it was least welcome.

Cara stirred against him and, when his arms slackened about her, she eased herself away from him. 'Tell me about Chantal?'

It was a sobering question, and one which she could not leave for later if she wanted total peace of mind, and Vince seemed to sense the urgency behind her query.

'I'm not going to deny that Chantal and I had a close relationship before I met you,' he confessed with an honesty she found almost touching. 'The purpose of her visit was to tell me that she had met someone whom she wanted to marry, and I was so happy for her that I confessed to her my feelings for you.'

'Knowing how you felt about me didn't stop her from behaving possessively towards you,' Cara pointed out, her jealousy returning with a vengeance.

'I had enlisted her aid to make you jealous in the hope of discovering whether you cared for me,' he explained, his fingers caressing her warm cheek. 'Were you jealous?'

'Murderously jealous,' she confessed, curling her fingers about his wrist and pressing her lips against his rough palm.

'That's good,' he ground out the words. 'I was jealous of John Curtis, and I felt like killing him that day when I walked into the library and found him there with you.'

Cara's eyes widened in astonishment. 'You had no reason to be jealous of him.'

'I knew how he felt about you, and that was enough,' he said in a clipped voice, getting to his feet and lifting her up with him. Cara felt bereft without his arms about her, and her eyes followed him curiously as he walked towards the fireplace to lean with his hands against the mantelshelf. He was frowning fiercely into the fire, and she was beginning to feel inordinately perturbed when he turned abruptly to face her. 'Can you ever forgive me for what I did to your father and to you?'

A tender smile curved her mouth as she joined him in front of the fireplace and, savouring the joyous freedom of seeking out his nearness, she slid her arms about his neck and leaned her body against his with a newfound confidence.

'Knowing and understanding makes it easy to forgive, Vince.' She raised her face to his and her expression sobered fractionally. 'Are you serious about helping my father?'

'Very serious.' His stern expression relaxed after a moment until his eyes glittered with a teasing smile. 'Weren't you the one who said that I can't live with hatred and revenge all my life?'

'I didn't think you would take any notice of what I said,' she laughed softly, leaning back against the circle of his arms to study his face.

Her laughter died on a faint gasp at what she saw in his eyes, and for endless, breathtaking seconds they both lifted the shutters to their souls. Their eyes spoke a language for which words were ineloquent, and Cara had the ecstatic feeling that she had been freed from the bondage of uncertainty.

'Cara, *liebchen*, I love you,' Vince murmured throatily as if he wanted to make sure she understood, then his hard mouth came down on hers.

The passionate demand of his kiss awakened a hunger which she could no longer suppress, and she responded with a surging warmth of her own. She felt Vince's thigh muscles grow taut against her own, and she knew his need as well as she knew her own.

They were reeling on the brink of desire when a sharp tap on the living-room door made them draw apart, and Cara could tell by the look on his face that he resented this intrusion as much as she did.

'Jackson has asked me to tell you that if he has to delay dinner much longer it will be ruined,' Harriet informed them from the doorway with a faintly amused smile on her lips.

'We're coming,' Vince told her, releasing a blushing Cara, but Harriet went out again and closed the door firmly behind her.

Vince's hands reached for Cara the moment they were alone, but that brief respite had allowed a very serious matter to leap to the surface of her mind.

'What about my father's loan?' she asked anxiously, avoiding Vince's arms.

'I shall be writing if off as atonement for the mental agony I have caused him.' Vince smiled down into her incredulous eyes. 'I can't have the father of the woman I love indebted to me financially, now can I?'

Cara felt the last fragment of tension disintegrate inside her, and her eyes were moist with happy tears as she drew Vince's head down to hers to kiss him on his lips. 'I think you're wonderful, and I adore you to distraction.'

The light that entered his eyes gave him that devilish look she was so accustomed to. 'Tell me that again when we are alone tonight . . . if you dare.'

Cara's soft laughter was unconsciously provocative when she linked her arm through his on their way to dinner. Later, when they were alone, she would rise to meet his challenge, and he knew it, but this time there would be no need to withhold from him that part of her which she had been too wary to disclose in the past.

Vince was a devil; and he could be a ruthless devil as well. He would never change entirely from the arrogant, often cruel man she had learned to love, but there was incredible joy in the discovery that he had a heart after all, and his heart belonged to her.

Coming Next Month in Harlequin Presents!

783 TROPICAL EDEN   Kerry Allyne
Against her wishes, a powerful development company bids on her
father's resort. And despite her engagement, she's drawn to the
arrogant usurper of her tropical Eden.

784 THE FIRE AND THE ICE   Vanessa James
Two years after penning a scathing article about a wealthy
playboy-editor, a reporter runs hot and cold when she finds herself
working for the man behind the myth.

785 THE ONLY ONE   Penny Jordan
For the rags-to-riches chairman of Hart Industries, the previous
owner of his fifteenth-century estate is elusively appealing,
fleetingly desirable at any price.

786 THE PASSIONATE LOVER   Carole Mortimer
An English heiress finds herself stranded in a Montana blizzard
then rescued—not by her concerned fiancé—but by his
arrogant, presumptuous cousin.

787 THE DAUGHTER OF NIGHT   Jeneth Murrey
A London hairdresser traces her natural mother to ask for help with
her foster parent's medical bills, only to be accused of blackmail
and subjected to a masterpiece of extortion, involving marriage!

788 TOTAL SURRENDER   Margaret Pargeter
An interior designer's boss might not desert her at the altar the
way her fiancé did. But she's afraid if she surrenders to his
determined seduction, he'll leave her alone and devastated.

789 NO GENTLE PERSUASION   Kay Thorpe
Desperation drives a daughter to plead her father's case with a
man she suspects will respond to no gentle persuasion. So she
confronts him with a shockingly blunt proposition....

790 CAPE OF MISFORTUNE   Yvonne Whittal
Dissatisfied with life in Durban, a teacher becomes the governess
at a tropical villa still reeling from the mystery surrounding the
death of her employer's wife.

EYE OF THE STORM

MAURA SEGER

A powerful
portrayal of
the events of
World War II in the
Pacific, *Eye of the Storm* is a riveting story of how love
triumphs over hatred. Aboard a ship steaming toward
Corregidor, Army Lt. Maggie Lawrence meets Marine Sgt.
Anthony Gargano. Despite military regulations against frater-
nization, they resolve to face together whatever lies ahead....
A searing novel by the author named by *Romantic Times* as
1984's Most Versatile Romance Author.

Take these
4 best-selling novels
FREE

Yes! Four sophisticated, contemporary love stories by four world-famous authors of romance FREE, as your introduction to the Harlequin Presents subscription plan. Thrill to **Anne Mather**'s passionate story BORN OUT OF LOVE, set in the Caribbean.... Travel to darkest Africa in **Violet Winspear**'s TIME OF THE TEMPTRESS....Let **Charlotte Lamb** take you to the fascinating world of London's Fleet Street in MAN'S WORLD....Discover beautiful Greece in **Sally Wentworth**'s moving romance SAY HELLO TO YESTERDAY.

 *The very finest in romance fiction*

Join the millions of avid Harlequin readers all over the world who delight in the magic of a really exciting novel. EIGHT great NEW titles published EACH MONTH! Each month you will get to know exciting, interesting, true-to-life people . . . . You'll be swept to distant lands you've dreamed of visiting . . . . Intrigue, adventure, romance, and the destiny of many lives will thrill you through each Harlequin Presents novel.

Get all the latest books before they're sold out!
As a Harlequin subscriber you actually receive your personal copies of the latest Presents novels immediately after they come off the press, so you're sure of getting all 8 each month.

Cancel your subscription whenever you wish!
You don't have to buy any minimum number of books. Whenever you decide to stop your subscription just let us know and we'll cancel all further shipments.